**1**

**M**OHAMMED Rashid Hamani died a happy and contented man. The April sun was shining brightly on the small piazza where he sat at a pavement table before one of the fashionable cafes. He had dined alone, but after six months in Rome he had formed a liking for Italian food and wine that had given him sufficient satisfaction. He had eaten well and he belched loudly before savouring the last sip of red *chianti* that still remained in his glass. He signalled a waiter and ordered coffee, and then lit up a black Turkish cigarette from a slim gold case. He leaned back in his chair like a potentate at ease, a swarthy but not unhandsome man, replete, and with nothing better to do than watch the girls go by.

They were beautiful, these Italian

girls, so many of them with sun-tanned limbs and full, voluptuous bosoms. Hamani derived pleasure simply from feasting his eyes. He liked the really lusty-looking girls, and especially those with dark and flashing eyes. A superb example approached him now and he reflected licentiously on the tasty shape of her full red mouth. With a mouth like that even a kiss would be ecstasy. The girl was looking straight ahead, not even aware that Hamani existed, and his mind became absorbed in the delicious mental task of peeling off her clothes. There was traffic swishing constantly through the piazza and so the sound of another car coming up fast did not distract him. The girl saw what Hamani would never see and the ripe red mouth opened suddenly in a horrified scream.

The sound of the submachine-gun hammered through the piazza and the burst of bullets smashed Hamani from his chair and pushed his body down and under the table as though he had been swept there by a blood-stained broom.

★ ★ ★

Sergeant Victor Bardini of the *Guardia Di Pubblica Sicurezza* sat at one of the tables of an almost identical cafe on the opposite side of the piazza. Bardini was twenty eight years old, efficient, athletic and intelligent, and while watching Hamani happily feeding he had become thoroughly bored with his job.

The Rome Police knew that Mohammed Rashid Hamani was one member of a group, suspected to be terrorists of the Palestine Liberation Army, who had infiltrated into Italy from France. It was hoped that the Arab would eventually lead them to his companions, but Hamani was aware that he was under surveillance and so far he had succeeded in eluding his shadows whenever he needed to make contact with his friends. The limitations

3

of manpower made it impossible to keep a round-the-clock-watch on every suspect, and so a hit or miss system had to be evolved. The police watch was frequently drawn off in the hope of lulling the Arab into a false sense of security, and then intensified for short, hopeful periods. It was a game as predictable as Russian roulette, and one that was played out between police and political criminals in every capital in Europe.

For the past two days Hamani had been under close observation, but Bardini felt sure that the Arab was aware that the heat had been turned up again. Hamani was either innocent, or clever enough to make no mistakes until the heat cooled, and so Bardini was gloomily confident that he was wasting his time.

The young Sergeant was occupying his mind in much the same manner as his quarry. He was watching the girls go by. However he did hear the sound of the approaching car, and because the pavement on his side of the piazza was temporarily empty of any particularly eye-worthy female form he idly turned his head. He saw the blue Lancia convertible sweep into the small square with two dark-faced, thick-nosed men inside. One man held the wheel while his companion raised the submachine-gun. The sound shocked the piazza into a frozen stillness. Then it was all over with Hamani dead and the blue Lancia disappearing before Bardini had fully grasped what was happening. When the echoes died away the girl on the far pavement was still screaming. She had never stopped.

Before that happened Bardini had moved. For a few blank seconds he had been as startled as anyone, but then he reacted quickly. His own car, a black Fiat 2300 coupé, was parked only yards away. He left another overturned table in his wake but he was inside the car and sliding behind the wheel only seconds after the blue Lancia had vanished from sight. The key dangled in the ignition, a routine precaution on a surveillance job when the car could be needed in a hurry. He switched on the engine, crashed the car into gear and roared off in pursuit.

Driving with one hand Bardini groped for his radio-telephone. He began to speak rapidly but effectively, cramming the maximum of information into a minimum of words, and then keeping up a running commentary of the chase.

The Lancia and the Fiat were evenly matched, each with a top speed of up to 110 m.p.h. On the open road the hundred yards start might have enabled the assassination car to pull slowly ahead, but in the traffic-crowded streets of Rome there was no chance. The driver of the Lancia had to constantly brake and swerve, and because Bardini could take advantage of the gaps already made he quickly had the open-topped blue convertible in sight.

The thick-nosed man in the passenger seat of the Lancia had pushed his submachine-gun down and out of sight. He twisted and looked back, expecting no trouble but unable to refrain from making sure. He saw the black Fiat coming up fast, still eighty yards behind. It was a plain car, but the grim-faced man behind the wheel had a radio microphone raised to his mouth and the implications were unmistakable. The thick-nosed man snapped a warning. His driver looked back briefly, cursed, and then jammed his foot hard down on the accelerator.

A small truck lumbered out of a side turning. The blue Lancia did a contorted dancing wriggle to get round the bonnet and hurtled on. The petrified truck driver skidded his vehicle to a halt in the middle of the road. Bardini dropped his radio-microphone to grab at the wheel with both hands. The Fiat mounted the pavement, clipped the back of the truck and all but nose-dived into a shop-front before Bardini could heave it back on to the road.

A set of traffic lights flashed up, an amber warning that quickly blazed red. The blue Lancia crashed through split seconds before the cross flow of traffic began shooting forward. Bardini followed with his horn blaring, causing a chaos of hastily applied brakes and skidding impacts. The Fiat zig-zagged through missing collisions by shaved seconds and Bardini was suddenly sweating.

The thick-nosed man looked back again and saw the Fiat still in pursuit. Panic gripped him and he hauled up the submachine-gun and rested it on the back of his seat. He rammed in a full magazine and then lifted the weapon to fire.

Bardini saw all the movements. Fear wanted him to brake but at the last moment he took a tyre-screaming turn left into a side street. The submachine-gun blazed a spray of bullets into the road he had just left.

Bardini kept his foot down and took

two right turns to bring him back to the main road. He had lost a hundred yards but the blue Lancia was still in sight. He drove like a madman to regain the lost ground, praying that the crazy killer with the submachine-gun did not have an unlimited supply of magazines.

Above the screaming of terrified pedestrians and the honking and screeching of frantic vehicles trying to get out of the way there came a new sound. A sound that was sweet relief to Victor Bardini. It was the siren of the first police car answering his urgent radio alert.

The two men in the Lancia also heard the approaching siren. Then they saw the flashing blue light on the white patrol car racing towards them. The patrol car braked fifty yards ahead and swung itself sideways to block the road. The driver of the Lancia cursed and braked, rubber shredding from his tyres as he howled to a stop. He began to back up rapidly until he could swing right into a side road. The two policemen from the patrol car jumped out with revolvers blazing. The man with the submachine-gun emptied his magazine to make them scatter. The stink of cordite joined with the stink of burnt rubber. The Lancia raced off again but by then Bardini had regained all his lost ground and the Fiat followed into the side road on two tortured wheels. The patrol car joined in the chase, again with its siren wailing its banshee cry.

In the next ten minutes the Lancia and the Fiat, together with the pack of converging patrol cars that joined in the hunt, caused between them a series of three major and twenty-seven minor accidents. The driver of the blue Lancia hammered his engine, brakes and gearbox in a mounting frenzy, twisting and turning with his curses rising fast into hysteria. The pack stayed on his tail and in their wake they left chaos and pandemonium, and a shambles of wrecked shop-fronts and vehicles.

The Lancia had only a minimal lead when it streaked blindly across the broad Piazza Venezia in the very heart of Rome. It passed before the magnificent white marble Alter of the Nation with its mounted golden figure of Victor Emmanuel and its crowning golden chariots gleaming in the sun. A multiple pile-up in the traffic-crowded square included two of the pursuing police cars, but as the Lancia all but overturned into the broad avenue of the Via Dei Fori Imperiali, Bardini's Fiat and two remaining police cars were still trailing only yards behind.

The Lancia led the way down the straight tree-shaded avenue at seventy miles per hour. The ancient ruins of the Forum flashed by in a blur and the great, ruined ampitheatre of the Colosseum sprang to meet them. Half way down the avenue two more police cars leaped out of the Via Cavour to tag on to the pursuit, and by the time the driver of the Lancia was braking before the Colosseum itself the massed wailing of police sirens had risen from a quartet to a full orchestra.

The way ahead was blocked by three white patrol cars slowly circling the Colosseum in a line abreast. The driver of the Lancia turned desperately to his right and aimed for the triumphal Arch of Constantine stradling the Via Gregorio. Through the triple archway he saw three more approaching police cars and was forced into another change of direction. He swung right again to continue round the Colosseum and crashed head on into another patrol car.

Bardini skidded his Fiat to a protesting stop and jumped out. He saw the driver of the Lancia stumble away and shouted. The man turned back and pulled an automatic from a shoulder holster. He fired and Bardini dropped flat beside the Fiat.

Bardini fumbled for his own gun and then wriggled underneath his car. The two dark-faced men were both moving away from their wrecked vehicle. The man with the submachine-gun was running ahead while the driver held back less certainly with his automatic. Bardini reached the opposite side of his car and poked his head out from behind the front wheel. The driver of the Lancia had decided that they had a personal vendetta to settle and fired again. The bullet hit the bodywork of the Fiat above Bardini's head with a clang like a sledge hammer in an echo chamber. Bardini's ears were ringing as he answered the shot. He aimed more carefully and the driver of the Lancia staggered back and fell sprawling.

It seemed as though every police car in Rome had descended upon the Colosseum, and the survivor of the assassination team had no choice of retreat except to duck into one of the brown stone archways into the great arena. Bardini stood up to follow but then another black Fiat skidded to a stop beside him. The man who got out was shorter and heavier than Bardini, but he had experience and authority.

He surveyed the scene with a glance.

"Easy now, Sergeant." Inspector Roberto Gaiani rested a restraining hand on Bardini's trembling shoulder. "If it is possible I want to take the second man alive."

★ ★ ★

Roberto Gaiani was more than a senior officer of the *Guardia Di Pubblica Sicurezza*. He was also the Rome Section Head for Counter-Terror, the European security organization established to deal exclusively with international terrorism and political crime. Counter-Terror, was in many ways a parallel of Interpol, plugging the vital political gap, which, by the very nature of its constitution, Interpol was obliged to leave wide open.

Gaiani took immediate command, using his hand radio to rap direct orders to all units. Unfortunately one running police officer stumbled and banged his chest hard against the stonework of an archway in his haste to get under cover. His personal radio was clipped into his breast pocket and the impact killed it stone dead. He failed to receive Gaiani's priority command.

There was no escape for the thick-nosed man with the submachine-gun. The Colosseum was surrounded on all sides by police vehicles, and as the tourists fled outwards in all directions so the lesser flood of police officers poured in.

The fugitive tried to circle the great ampitheatre in the cavernous shadows beneath the tiers. He saw police uniforms ahead and more police officers infiltrating warily through practically every archway. He had to turn inwards, backing through another arch that brought him back into bright sunlight in the centre of the arena. Like the doomed gladiators who had preceded him here two thousand years before he saw no choice but to fight out his own bloody battle to the death. He turned and pressed his back against the guard rail that prevented tourists from falling into the central excavations and quickly changed the magazines on his submachine-gun. The full magazine that he rammed home was the last.

It was a short and vicious battle. At the first sight of a police uniform the thick-nosed man opened fire. The police officers fired back, aiming low at his legs. The trapped man ran round the inside of the arena but more police officers appeared in the archways on the far side The fugitive turned desperately through the nearest archway that would take him back beneath the tiers of ruined seats. He saw a movement in the gloom as a short, heavy man dodged from one archway to the next. He blazed away with submachine-gun, but half blinded by the transition from glaring sunlight to deep shadow he missed. Roberto Gaiani crouched behind a buttress of grey black stone and shot the thick-nosed man accurately two inches above the left knee.

The police officer who had lost radio contact appeared on the opposite side of the arena in the same moment. He saw the man with the submachine-gun spraying bullets into the far archway and swiftly raised his own revolver. The bullet scored a fatal hit.

Gaiani lowered his own automatic with satisfaction as he saw his target stagger to a stop. The thick-nosed man stared down at the red hole above his knee. Then he seemed to lean over backwards and his face contorted again. He crumpled and fell, and Gaiani's satisfaction turned to anger as he realized that someone had either disobeyed or misunderstood his orders. Shouting to the rest of his men to hold their fire he ran forward with Bardini at his side.

★ ★ ★

The man who had murdered Mohammed Rashid Hamani was dying fast in his turn, his life ebbing with the pool

17

of dark lung blood that was forming beneath his right shoulder blade. He was still conscious and his eyes were open but his vision was glazed.

Gaiani crouched beside him and asked softly, "Who are you?"

There was no answer. Gaiani was sure that his voice had been heard for the dark, pain-dulled eyes were trying to focus on his face. He realized that in the mind of the dying man there was no need to answer, there was no will to make an effort. Gaiani had to change that and there was no time to waste.

"Listen to me," Gaiani said urgently. "You are not able to talk so I will make guesses. The man you killed, Mohammed Hamani, was a member of a Palestine Liberation group. You know that — that is why you killed him! You are also from the Middle East, and as you are an enemy of the Arabs it is obvious that you must be a Jew. Your name does not matter, but you are an Israeli agent of the *Shinbeth*."

The man said nothing, there was no hint of admission or denial, but Gaiani knew that his logic must be right.

"I am not asking you to betray your friends," Gaiani persisted. "Only your enemies. You must have knowledge about Hamani and his group — that information you can and must reveal to me!"

The thick-nosed man smiled faintly, a bitter acknowledgement that he did have such information, even though he was not prepared to share it.

"In a very few minutes you will be dead," Gaiani said slowly. "That is not my wish, it is an unpleasant fact. It is impossible for you to make a report back to your friends of the *Shinbeth*. The knowledge you have is wasted if it dies with you. If you want any further action taken against your enemies then you must talk to me."

"Why?" A spasm of agony creased the dying man's face. He forced more words out and the first bubbles of blood spilled through his weakly moving lips.

"Why should I help the men who have killed me?"

"Because your enemies are our enemies," Gaiani said simply. "I regret that you have lost your life, but you knew the risks when you chose to fight your secret war on my territory. Now only I can continue your fight, and only if you talk."

The *Shinbeth* man looked slowly round the blurred circle of faces that crouched above him. All that he wanted now was to die in peace. He knew instinctively that the next effort he made to speak would kill him.

Bardini leaned close. "You killed the man who was our only lead," he said carefully. "We know that Hamani had three companions in Paris. We believe that those three men are also in Rome and that with Hamani they were plotting some new act of terrorism. Tell us where they can be found."

Gaiani realized that the thick-nosed man was on the very brink of death and that even if he found the will he would not have the time to give them anything substantial.

"Just a name," Gaiani begged. "You have killed the only man we know. Give us another name."

There was a long silence. The *Shinbeth* man closed his eyes. He was never to open them again, but briefly he unlocked his lips.

"The group leader," he said faintly. "Hasan Bakarat. Number twenty-five, Via Ventura."

The last word was almost unaudible and with it he expired.

# 2

IN the apartment room above the Via Ventura the curtains had been drawn to shut out the bright sunlight. The semi-darkness softened the bare and shabby nature of the room, which had only two occupants. The only sounds were the ticking of the clock, the strained creaking of the bed, the grunts of the man and the excruciating moans of the woman. The bout of feverish movement ended with an animal gasping and a long, shuddering cry. Then the man and the woman subsided into stillness and silence and only the ticking of the clock remained.

After a few moments Sonia Rocco opened her eyes. She was bathed in sweat, her own and her lover's, and in this moment there was always a tinge of shame. She looked up at the dark, cruel face above her, a face with a hawk nose and fierce eyes. Hasan Bakarat smiled, but it was a smile without tenderness. He was never gentle with her. Sonia wondered often why she stayed with this man who hurt her as much as he pleased her.

She knew very little about this man who called himself Hasan Bakarat, except that he was strong and lean and physically fit. He was a hard, forceful man, not only with sex but with all his dealings with other people. Sometimes she sensed the bitter, driving anger that simmered inside him and then she was afraid. Her fear was always accompanied in some strange way by a vague feeling of compassion, as though she understood that even this black and terrible anger was in some way justified. He had told her that his home was Algeria and that he had come to Rome to look for work, but she was sure that both statements were lies. He had never again talked of Algeria and he had never looked for work.

Bakarat wondered what she was thinking, if anything. He guessed that she wanted him to move, to relieve her of his weight, but he preferred to keep her pinned down beneath him. His right hand moved over her bare shoulder to her breast. The movement was slow but it was not a caress. He squeezed and Sonia gasped with the pain. His finger and thumb closed over the still swollen nipple and he twisted carefully. Tears flooded her eyes and she reached for him with frantic kisses. Complete submission was her only defence to his commanding strength and with that he was satisfied.

Once Bakarat's most burning ambition had been to achieve the rape and humiliation of a Jewish girl. Then he had decided that an English or an American girl would serve just as well. Finally his hatred had increased until it included any girl who had not been born in the living hell of a refugee camp. The black anger that was the core of his being had taken a more practical direction, and so he could afford some relaxation of his personal ambitions. So Sonia Rocco now served his sexual needs well enough.

Sonia was still trying to placate him with her abandoned kisses when they heard a violent knocking on the outer door. Bakarat swore and then rolled off the girl and the bed. He walked through into the second half of the apartment, a cramped kitchen and dining room.

"Who is there?" he demanded irritably.

"Farraj." The voice was hoarse and urgent.

"Go away. I am busy."

"It is important, Hasan. I must see you now."

Bakarat became aware of the undercurrent of agitation and alarm that ran through his friend's tone. Also he realized that Farraj would never come here uninvited and in broad daylight without good reason. He frowned and then opened the door. Farraj, a short, dark bullfrog of a man squeezed inside before Bakarat could step back, almost pushing him out of the way. Farraj was breathless and looked badly shaken.

"Wait here," Bakarat said sharply.

He turned and went back into the bedroom to pick up his trousers and shirt. "Get dressed," he told Sonia curtly, and then he left her again and closed the door behind him.

"Now." He looked at Farraj, his eyes warning the other man to keep his voice low. "What is wrong?"

"Hamani is dead," Farraj told him bitterly.

Bakarat stopped in the act of pulling on his trousers. He stared, shock numbing his brain only briefly before he demanded:

"Hamani dead? How? When?"

"Only a few minutes ago. I just received a telephone call from a waiter at the restaurant. He said that Hamani was sitting at one of the pavement tables. A car went past with two men inside. They shot him dead with a submachine-gun."

"You say two men in a car — the *Shinbeth*?"

"Who else?" There were bitter tears in Farraj's eyes. "What other organization is there that hunts down and murders the sons of Palestine?"

Bakarat felt fury, first blazing hot and then freezing cold, washing over him in succeeding waves. Then his brain took command and he zipped up his trousers and buckled his belt.

"If Hamani is dead then we must leave Rome," he decided grimly.

"First we must avenge our friend. We must have blood for blood."

"No!" Bakarat snapped. "We know that our friend Hamani was being watched by the Rome Police. Now that he has been assassinated the police will need no other excuse to search his rooms. They may find something that will lead them here."

"They will find nothing. Hamini was a clever man. And he was our brother — we owe him vengeance."

"We have a mission," Bakarat

reminded him. "Everything is planned and ready. We have spent six months in the planning and this time we cannot fail. We were due to leave Rome in two days time, so now we will advance our departure by two days and leave immediately. Get to a telephone and call Shefik. Tell him to meet us at the airport."

"I can go to Hamani's rooms," Farraj argued. "If I go now I can be there before the police. If there is anything to lead them here I can destroy it. Then we will have two days before we leave Rome on schedule. We can kill many Jews in two days. Any Jew will do."

"The risk is too great. Everything you suggest will jeopardise our mission." Bakarat seized the shoulders of his friend and his voice shook with passion. "I promise you, Ferraj, that if I am alive after our main task is finished, then I will dedicate myself to vengeance for our friend Hamani — but until then the main task must be our priority."

Farraj stared at him for a long, anguished minute, and then he nodded slowly and gave way.

"You are right, Hasan. This is what Hamani would want also. I will telephone Shefik."

Bakarat urged his friend to hurry and after another minute was able to hustle him out of the apartment. When Farraj had gone Bakarat put on his shirt and went back into the bedroom. Sonia Rocco was sitting on the bed. She had put on her clothes and now she was nervously applying fresh lipstick. Her eyes were worried and she stopped in mid-movement.

"Hasan, what is happening?" Bakarat frowned. He had not yet told her that he had intended to leave, but now this sudden emergency made it easier.

"There is some trouble," he said brusquely. "Not serious, but it means that I must leave Rome for a few weeks. You must leave now — go home and do not come back to this

29

place. When I return to Rome I will find you."

Sonia asked bewildered questions. Bakarat cut them short and gave her no answers. He pulled her close and kissed her hard. Then he pushed her through the door.

"Go now, and remember that you must not come back. When it becomes possible I will come to you."

Sonia did not know whether she could believe him or not, but she did know that it would be futile to argue. Helplessly, almost in a daze, she left the apartment.

★ ★ ★

The prolonged pursuit of the blue Lancia and then the surrounding of the Colosseum and the drama within had all taken time, and so it was an hour later before the black Fiat 2300 swept up the Via Ventura and stopped before number twenty-five. Victor Bardini was again at the wheel but now Roberto

30

Gaiani was beside him. There were back-up forces within easy call but as yet Gaiani did not want to flood the Via Venturo with police cars and uniforms. One violent gun battle was enough for the day and he hoped to avoid another. He and Bardini were in plain clothes so he had decided that they would make the initial approach alone.

They got out of the car without haste and entered the building. It was a four storey apartment block and a brief word with an enquiring caretaker on the ground floor informed them that the only tenant of obvious Arab origin was the occupant of number B-3 on the third floor. The two police officers calmly ascended the twisting staircase and then positioned themselves on either side of the suspect door. They produced automatics and listened. There was silence. Gaiani knocked.

There was no movement from inside the apartment. Gaiani waited for a

31

moment and then knocked again, this time more loudly. Again there was no response.

Before leaving the caretaker Gaiani had politely commandeered her keys. Now he silently fitted a key into the lock. The third key that he tried turned the tumblers with a sharp click. Swiftly Gaiani turned the doorknob and pushed. Bardini kicked the door wide and they went through together. They separated left and right, each man moving into a fast, defensive crouch.

They felt slightly foolish as they knelt in the empty kitchen. Gaiani stood up slowly and Bardini followed his example. They approached the bedroom door and again Bardini kicked it open. Inside the tension gave way to frustration and anti-climax and they relaxed. The automatics were returned to shoulder holsters. Gaiani looked down on the soiled and rumpled bed and wrinkled his nose with distaste.

"He left in a hurry," Bardini said

wryly. He stopped and picked up a tissue paper stained with lipstick and added, "So did his woman."

Gaiani pulled back the curtains and opened a window. Then he used his radio and called in the rest of the men that he would need.

The two rooms of the apartment were searched thoroughly but the search revealed nothing. Hasan Bakarat had not left his old habitat clean, but he had stripped it of everything that might have given a clue to his future movements. After twenty fruitless minutes Gaiani was ready to move on and start questioning the other inhabitants of the building, and then a call came over his radio. Gaiani acknowledged and paused to listen.

"Inspector Gaiani, we have a report from Sergeant Raimondo. The apartment of the dead man Mohammed Hamani has been investigated as you ordered. Raimondo has discovered a passport in the name of Mohammed Rashid Hamani which has been stamped with an entry visa for Spain. With the passport there was an airline ticket to Madrid, plus brand new Spanish currency notes to the equivalent of two hundred thousand lira."

"Contact the airport," Gaiani snapped promptly. "I want a full security clampdown on all flights to Madrid.

★ ★ ★

The request reached Rome's Leonardo da Vinci International Airport four minutes too late, for by that time Flight 379 of Iberia Spanish Airlines was already airborne with Bakarat and his two companions aboard. They were in luck because the flight time was convenient and there had been several vacant seats. Their passports were all in order and so there had been no difficulty in changing the dates on their tickets. The pretty Spanish girl at the airport reception desk had barely listened to Bakarat's hastily invented explanations for their sudden change of schedule. Her job was simply to smile sweetly, and wherever possible to oblige.

When Roberto Gaiani heard the news he could only fume and run an exasperated hand through his greying hair. There were established Counter-Terror offices in the police departments in Paris, Munich and London, and more recently the network had been expanded to include Zurich, Vienna, Brussels and Amsterdam, but as yet there was no Counter-Terror office in Madrid.

★ ★ ★

The Hotel Carmen in a quiet back street in the old quarter of Madrid was a somewhat dilapidated place that had seen better days. It's rooms were rarely fully booked and so although Bakarat and his two companions arrived forty-eight hours earlier than they were expected there was no difficulty in providing them with accommodation.

They had two extra days in the Spanish capital and so they used it to recover their nerve. None of them were fully aware of how narrow their escape had been, but they had all been shaken to some degree by the abrupt death of their friend Hamani.

Shefik and Farraj drank heavily and plotted bloody vengeance. Shefik was a thin-faced fire-eater full of nervous tension, a man to whom waiting was a cross and patience most definitely not a virtue. Their wild schemes for action when the main task was over finally incensed Bakarat who exploded and lashed them with his tongue. They had to concentrate on one job at a time he warned them furiously. If they allowed the death of Hamani to distract their minds from the main task then they would fail. The main task was a priority which must take precedence over the life or death of any individual involved and so they must not fail. This time he, Hasan Bakarat, vowed that they would succeed.

They almost came to blows, but then Shefik and Farraj accepted grudgingly that Bakarat was right. The reminder of their previous failures raised their gall, but it also restored the grim determination with which they had planned and argued the details of their present operation over the past six months.

For the rest of their enforced stay in Madrid they were sullen and mostly silent. The strain of waiting would have worn on their nerves at this stage even without the death of Hamani on their minds. Mostly they stayed in their rooms and played cards, but they were unable to concentrate. Shefik and Farraj continued to drink but Bakarat was determined to stay sober. Again and again he lectured them with memories of the refugee camps, reminding them of the wretched, hopeless misery of their people which they knew so well. Again and again he told them that they were a handful of commandos fighting a war — a war in which the whole world was a battlefield, and in which every man who was not their sworn friend was an enemy. Again and again he drilled and coached them on the duty they had to perform.

On the fourth day the telephone rang on schedule. Bakarat answered with relief and confirmed a pre-planned rendezvous.

After that Bakarat took no chances. He did not know whether a search of Hamani's apartment could have revealed anything that would put the Rome Police on his trail. Neither could he guess at what kind of liaison there might be between the Italian and Spanish Police. He only knew that it was not impossible for his group to be under observation and so he played safe.

The three men left their hotel together and then split up, Farraj walking away in one direction and Shefik and Bakarat in another. After a hundred yards it would have appeared to any observer that Bakarat had changed his mind. He returned to the hotel, leaving Shefik to continue alone. Having set up his two friends as decoys Bakarat then left the hotel again via the back fire escape. Even then he did not go direct to the appointed meeting place, but instead spent the next two hours in changing buses and taxis and generally zig-zagging about Madrid.

It was late afternoon when he finally entered the vast El Retiro Park and by then he was certain that he could not have been followed. He glanced at his wrist watch and hurried along the tree shaded paths until he reached a small blue lake that sparkled in the setting sun. The green peace of the park had attracted a number of visitors, and one of them was a young Japanese who was standing by the lakeside and sighting a choice of views through an expensive Nikon camera.

Bakarat approached the Japanese more slowly and stood beside him for a moment as though admiring the lake. Then he said softly,

"No justice for Palestine — "

" — No peace for the world." Koiso Takaaki completed their vow, and then he looked at Bakarat and smiled.

They shook hands warmly. Their initial exchange had been an affirmation rather than an introduction for they knew each other well. They had plotted together in Paris.

Koiso Takaaki was barely out of university, a slim, earnest young man who wore plain spectacles on a shining moon face. His placid appearance was a colossal deception for the new militant breed of Japanese youth had yet to spawn any man more fanatical. Takaaki was a dedicated Communist thinker on the Chinese pattern, and a leading member of Japan's underground Red Star Army, an organization violently opposed to Western Capitalism in all its forms. The Red Star Army also considered the whole Western world as its enemy and had formed a ready alliance with the extremists of the Palestine

40

Liberation movements. Together the two groups waged a ceaseless war of terror.

Bakarat and Takaaki exchanged news, smiling and talking rapidly.

"My group have all arrived in Spain." Takaaki informed the slightly taller Arab. "Yotaro has been living in Barcelona for the past three months, and he has the weapons and everything else that we need. The consignment came by sea and there was no trouble."

"Good." Bakarat approved. "But what news of our target?"

Takaaki smiled, "Our target left Kharg Island on schedule. Also the *Rhineland* sailed from Hamburg this morning. I have been keeping a careful watch on all the shipping news. Everything is proceeding to our plan. Hayashi and Odusu have found us a fishing boat that is possibly suitable for our purposes. They left last night to make the final arrangements. Your group must

41

be ready to move as soon as they send word."

"We are ready," Bakarat said. And he clenched a hard fist in a gesture of solidarity.

# 3

THE London office for Counter-Terror was situated in New Scotland Yard and here two worried men sat and pondered over the long report that had reached them from Gaiani in Rome. Detective Chief Superintendent Mark Nicolson, a tall fair-haired man in his late thirties was the London Section Head. His companion; Sir Alexander Gwynne-Vaughan, K.B.E., D.S.O., a large, straight-backed man with iron-grey hair and a clipped white moustache, had the unenviable job of Co-ordinator over all sections.

The police officers seconded to Counter-Terror were all active investigating officers in their own countries, but the bulk of their work concerned the stuy and circulation of all possible information on the movements of suspected terrorists. Gaiani's detailed report reached Mark Nicolson's desk as a matter of routine, just as exact copies reached the desks of Major Paul Cassin in Paris, Inspector Max Brenner in Munich, and the Counter-Terror offices in other capitals of Europe.

"Is there anything from your friend Ramondez?" Nicolson asked.

"Nothing positive as yet," Gwynne-Vaughan frowned as he spoke. "Juan Ramondez is a good police officer and I'm confident that if we ever get the approval of the Franco Government he'll make an excellent Counter-Terror Section Head for Madrid. Unfortunately, until that happens, he can only oblige us semi-officially in his own time. We know that our three Arabs have gone to earth in Madrid. Given a free hand, a properly functioning office and a handful of good men, Ramondez would soon find them. As things are he has no such resources or authority. Instead he has a normal police officer's work load of routine crime cases. He had promised to help us as far as he

44

is able, but it would be a mistake to expect miracles."

"It's a pity that your negotiations in Madrid fell through," Nicolson remarked gloomily.

"I haven't completely given up hope." Gwynne-Vaughan smiled wryly. "As soon as possible I intend to start a second round of talks with their Ministry of Home Affairs. The problems are difficult because Spain has no real need to become a part of the Counter-Terror network. To date there have been no serious terrorist attacks on Spain from our usual Arab sources. It's true that the shadow war of assassinations that has been raging all over Europe between Israeli and Arab agents has briefly touched Madrid. Two Arab gunmen shot down a *Shinbeth* man in the street in January of 1973 — but there has been nothing on the scale of the Olympic village slaughter in Munich, or the massacres at the Rome and Tel Aviv airports."

"So Spain does not face an Arab

terrorist threat to the same degree as the rest of Europe," Nicholson acknowledged. "But she does have her own internal problems."

"Precisely, and this is why my diplomatic efforts reached deadlock. Spain has a liberation movement amongst its own Basque population in the north — but Spain is a dictatorship which permits only one political party, where all liberal and leftwing movements are deliberately suppressed, and where Trade Unions are declared illegal. The Generalissimo's autocratic stand has even brought him into direct conflict with the Pope!"

"What you're saying is that Spain is the odd man out in a basically democratic Europe," Nicolson qualified bluntly. "Spain will have no interest in protecting the rest of us from Arab attacks, but she will attempt to use Counter-Terror as an extended arm of her own secret police."

Gwynne-Vaughan nodded. "That's our position exactly. In dealing with

Spain we're foundering on the very rock that Interpol sought to avoid by refusing to handle any politically motivated enquiry in the terms of its constitution. If Spain becomes part of the Counter-Terror network we could spend half of our time following up enquiries after outlawed Spanish trade unionists and dissentient Spanish priests. The real job of providing Europe with security cover from terrorist attacks will suffer from wasted time and manpower."

"And if Spain stays out she becomes a possible springboard for those attacks — a free territory where men like Bakarat can plot in safety, or retreat from surveillance."

Again Gwynne-Vaughan nodded grimly. "Those are the twin horns of our dilemma, and there is no easy solution. I have hopes that at some stage we will be able to establish a Counter-Terror office in Madrid, and in the meantime we can only hope that my contact and friendship with Juan Ramondez will prove fruitful."

As the Co-ordinator finished speaking a knock sounded on the door. They were expecting company and so Nicolson answered promptly. The door opened and the blunt face of Detective Sergeant First Class Harry Stone appeared.

"Inspector Helders has just arrived, sir," Stone said smartly.

"In the meantime," Gwynne-Vaughan added ruefully, "we also have problems in Amsterdam."

"But they are under control," assured a deep, gutteral but genial voice.

Harry Stone stood aside to admit a big, fat man who could only be described as ugly. His face would have fitted a Chicago gangster but his battered grin radiated a warmth of natural humour that made him immediately likeable.

Gwynne-Vaughan stood up to welcome the new arrival and then turned back to Nicolson.

"Mark, I don't think you've yet had the pleasure of meeting our new Section Head for Amsterdam — Inspector Dirk

Helders of the Dutch State Police."

"Welcome to the club, Inspector."

Nicolson stood up, betraying a slight limp in his left leg as he moved round the desk to shake hands.

When the introductions were complete they made themselves comfortable again. They talked generally for a few minutes, getting to know each other, and then Gwynne-Vaughan asked more seriously:

"How are things in Amsterdam?"

"My new office is functioning with reasonable smoothness," Helders said carefully. "As yet we are not contributing very much, but the information reports from the other Counter-Terror offices are flowing in and our filing system is taking shape. I have the full co-operation of our Minister of Justice, and I have a good working relationship with a number of senior officers of the *Marechaussee* — as you know they are responsible for patrolling our frontiers and manning immigration controls." He paused and pulled a comic face. "It would all be so much easier if

I was not saddled at the same time with the security arrangements for this coming conference."

Nicolson and Gwynne-Vaughan understood. The city of Amsterdam was currently playing host to the latest round of talks between delegates from N.A.T.O. and the Warsaw Pact. The subject was Mutual and Balanced Force Reductions, and the aim was to scale down the vast standing armies and ground forces that both sides maintained without altering the present balance of power. The cold war was slowly thawing and the two great power blocs of Europe were looking forward to peace instead of military conflict. The talks provided hope for the future, but for the present the safety of nineteen delegations of high ranking foreign diplomats provided a gigantic security headache for Holland.

"We'll give you all the help that we can," Gwynne-Vaughan promised. "If there is any movement of possible terrorists through Europe towards

Holland you will be warned."

"Can you forsee any possible threat?" Helders asked.

"There is nothing definite at the moment," Nicolson admitted. "Although I could advise you to watch all flights from Madrid for a man named Bakarat."

Helders laughed. "Have no fear, we shall be watching all flights from anywhere for anyone with an Arab name."

They moved on to a long discussion on the security details for the conference, and the problem of Hasan Bakarat and the lack of co-operation from the Spanish police receded into the background. Spain was safely separated from Holland by France and Belgium where efficient co-operation did exist, and that was comforting knowledge.

★ ★ ★

On the day following Bakarat's conversation with Koiso Takaaki in

Retiro Park the three Arabs left their hotel in Madrid. However, they did not go to the international airport, instead they went to the main railway station and separately booked train tickets to the northern city of Zaragoza. The journey took five dusty hours and they arrived in the heat of the afternoon. They were in haste now and had neither the time nor intention of viewing the city. Farraj and Shefik waited in a bar while Bakarat hunted for a garage and eventually hired an innocuous Peugeot saloon. He paid a heavy cash deposit to cover two weeks motoring and told the proprietor that he was heading for Barcelona. In actual fact he and his friends were bound in the opposite direction.

They left Zaragoza without delay. Their visit had simply been a feint, the cause of a number of grumbles from Shefik and Farraj, but made necessary by the cautious nature of Bakarat. He was the group leader and again he was taking no chances with the fear that they might be under police surveillance. He had learned that at every stage it was wise to twist, turn, twist again and then cover his tracks.

They drove all through the night, taking turns at the wheel and making only a minimum of essential stops. Their route passed through Logrono, Burgos, Leon and Orense, taking them in as direct a line as possible to the Atlantic Ocean. After passing through Orense Bakarat took the wheel again and turned north towards Cape Finisterre, the most north-westerly point of the Iberian Peninsular. Farraj now studied the map and gave careful directions.

On a wild mountain road leading to the coast Bakarat finally braked the Peugeot to a slow stop. He pulled in behind a dark green Mercedes that was parked and waiting and smiled broadly at his two companions.

Koiso Takaaki and another Japanese climbed out of the green Mercedes and walked to meet them.

"You are in good time," Takaaki said happily. "We do not move until darkness and there are several hours of daylight left."

★ ★ ★

The second Japanese was introduced as Jiro Yotaro. He too wore spectacles but he was a few inches shorter than Takaaki and a few years older. The stiff, upright spikes of his hair had greyed prematurely.

"Yotaro is our genius with electronics and radio communications," Takaaki informed the three Arabs. He indicated two large suitcases that had been transferred from the Mercedes to the Peugeot. "Here are our weapons — and the other is our gift to world peace."

They all laughed at the joke.

★ ★ ★

When dusk came they moved. The Mercedes was driven up a lonely gorge

54

out of sight and abandoned. Then the two Japanese crowded into the Peugeot with the three Arabs. Bakarat took the wheel and drove on until a bend in the road brought them out through a gap in the mountains. They looked down into a rugged bay where the black waves of the Atlantic heaved themselves angrily against the rocks. Rain, spray and wind mixed in the air, and far below near the mouth of the bay the lights of a small fishing village glowed faintly.

"Down there." Takaaki pointed.

Bakarat swung the wheel and the Peugeot followed the winding road down into the bay.

"The fishing boat is called the *Beatriz*," Takaaki informed them calmly. "She is moored at the end of the harbour wall and our friends Odusu and Hayashi are already on board. Odusu speaks Spanish and he has persuaded the two simpletons who own the boat to take himself and Hayashi out on a fishing trip. Their story is that they are journalists who are combining a holiday tour of Europe with the writing of a number of articles for a Japanese magazine. Odusu has paid well for the trip so the fishermen have not asked too many questions. The *Beatriz* is fuelled and ready and waiting to put to sea."

While Takaaki talked Yotaro opened up one of his suitcases and handed out Schmeisser machine pistols to each man. The weapons were the German World War Two equivalent to the British Sterling, readily available on the arms markets of the world and still as formidable as anything of more recent production. The 9mm ammunition was equally plentiful and Yotaro issued full magazines which were quickly clipped into place.

It was raining heavily as they passed through the shuttered village and the cobbled streets were deserted. The weather was in their favour and that gave Bakarat confidence. He was smiling as he turned on to the short stone breakwater that poked out into the bay and he stopped the car at the far end. They all got out, ignoring the rain and the sullen crashing of the waves that broke against the piled rocks on the seaward side of the wall. Instead they looked down dubiously at the thirty-five foot fishing boat with a single wheelhouse aft. The *Beatriz* barely looked big enough to take them all, but at this stage it was too late to change a single step in their plans.

Bakarat and Takaaki cocked their machine pistols and went on board.

The two fishermen who owned the boat were Giovanni Vasquez, a weather-beaten man of forty with a thin, sallow face, and his son Luis who was still in his teens. There was a microscopic cabin under the wheelhouse and here they were arguing in exasperation with their two paying guests who had spent the past twenty minutes in inventing excuses to delay sailing.

By now Vasquez was sorely tempted to throw these two peculiar little yellow men off his boat, despite the generous cash deal that had been arranged. First they wanted to sail with him and now they did not! The weather was too bad but they could not postpone their trip until a better night! They must go now, but not yet — what in the name of the Virgin Mary did they want he demanded angrily. The sound of his own raised voice prevented him from hearing the footsteps on the rain-lashed deck above, and the black muzzle of a machine pistol was touching the back of his neck before he realized that he had unexpected company.

After that he no longer had any free choice in the course of the night's events.

Yotaro's sophisticated luggage was brought aboard and stowed below, safe from spray and rain. Then Farraj drove the hired Peugeot a short distance into the hills and abandoned it in the first concealed spot. He returned to the harbour at a trot and arrived soaking wet and panting hoarsely for breath. The moment that he was back on board the *Beatriz* the helpless Vasquez and his terrified son were ordered to cast off.

Farraj noted that in his absence Hayashi and Odusu had also been armed with the Schmeisser machine pistols, and that in addition all four Japanese now wore long samurai swords slung across their shoulders.

The commandeered fishing boat headed its lifting bows towards the dark, rain-blurred mouth of the bay and the heaving breakers of the invisible Atlantic beyond. At six knots and in three hours they would be in the main sea lanes eighteen miles off Cape Finisterre.

The long-planned operation had begun.

# 4

THE *Rhineland* was a ten thousand ton German freighter, seventy hours out of Hamburg and bound for Freetown with a mixed cargo of heavy machinery, textiles and manufactured goods. She had enjoyed a smooth passage across the often temperamental Bay of Biscay, and only now as she approached the coast of Spain did she encounter seas heavy enough to make her pitch and groan to an uncomfortable degree. Eric Weber stood with his feet apart on the bridge and watched the curtain of rain streaking the windows. Visibility was almost nil beyond and he hoped that nothing too ferocious was blowing up out of the West. The *Rhineland* was an old ship with no stabilizers and in rough weather she rolled like a sick cow.

Weber yawned with boredom and wished that he was anywhere except at sea. The single gold bars on his shoulders identified him as the ship's Third Officer, but in fact he had nothing to do with the running of the ship and time dragged. This was only his second trip aboard the *Rhineland* and he had no previous experience at sea. His secret was supposed to be known only to Captain Schreiber and First Officer Muller, but by now Weber was convinced that anyone on board with above average intelligence must have their own suspicions. It hardly mattered because he was also beginning to believe that his presence here was a waste of time. He had hopes that this trip would be his last.

Eight bells rang. Weber had not heard Muller give the order but he was relieved. Midnight meant the end of their watch and he could go below. He waited with Muller until the change-over was made. The helmsman and the two seamen who had been standing by as messengers and lookouts handed over their positions to new men. Then Kesseler, the Second Officer, appeared to take command.

"Good morning, Herr Kesseler." The time was now twenty seconds past midnight and Muller was a stiff-necked man who was always formal and correct. "Your position is zero-nine-point-fifty degrees north by forty-two-point-seventy-five degrees west — and your course is south by east. The wind is south west, force six, and steady. We should reach Vigo in five hours, but Captain Schreiber will relieve you at four bells to take the ship into port. Any questions?"

"No, everything is clear," Kesseler confirmed. "Then you have command of the bridge."

Muller and Weber went below. Kesseler idly checked the chart, the binnacle and the radar scanner. Then he relaxed.

★ ★ ★

Weber went down to his cabin and took a five minute shower prior to turning into his bunk. When he had towelled himself dry he combed his hair back into its usual sleek blonde wave. He was a handsome young man of twenty-six with clear blue eyes and stripped he revealed a trim physique that knew the benefit of hard physical training to keep it in peak condition. Helga always called him her own *Tanhauser*, the minstrel knight of German legend who had been immortalized by Wagner.

The memory of Helga brought an immediate ache to his loins. It was only seventy-five hours since they had made love and already it seemed like eternity. He wondered how these full-time sailors could spend all their lives at sea. All he wanted was to get back to Hamburg, hoping that when this voyage ended he would see the last of the *Rhineland* and the end of his career at sea. Then Helga had promised to marry him at the first opportunity.

He cleaned his teeth and then donned

a pair of pyjamas before climbing into his bunk. The ship was rolling and he hoped that the motion would not get any worse. With luck they would be in Vigo before the storm broke. Their first port of call had little to offer, but at least it was shelter from the open sea. Weber switched off his light and fell asleep, dreaming erotically of Helga.

It seemed that the sharp knocking on the cabin door sounded immediately, although when he roused himself and looked at his wristwatch he saw that half an hour had passed. Reluctantly he switched on the light.

"The door is open," he called out lazily.

A face appeared, and he recognized one of the two seamen who formed the present duty watch.

"Captain Schreiber's compliments, Herr Weber," the man said formally. "He would like to see you on the bridge as soon as possible."

Weber stared. He was a discreet passenger and not a navigating officer and so the request was unprecedented. Then he recalled that this was Kesseler's watch. If Kesseler had good reason to wake up the Captain and the Captain was now calling for his psuedo Third Officer, then something unusual was happening.

Weber decided to ask no questions but quickly dressed and followed the seaman.

When he reached the bridge he found that Muller had also been recalled. The Captain and both his senior officers were grouped around the radar scanner. Weber joined them.

Schreiber turned his head. He was a stocky, bullet-headed man of few words.

"Do you speak Spanish?" he demanded.

"No, sir," Weber answered.

The Captain frowned. "We are picking up a distress call," he explained. The voice is in Spanish, very weak, and all that we can understand is the international codeword *Mayday*. The rest is just an unintelligible gabble."

Weber could not offer any useful comment. He stared down at the radar screen, watching the steady rotations of the illuminated radial line. On each pass the line was leaving just one bright spot forward and a little to the left of the centre of the screen. "That is the only vessel in our immediate vicinity, Muller said. "About three miles on our port bow."

"A small vessel," Schreiber qualified. "It must be a fishing boat or a small yacht." He looked to Kesseler. "Change our course two degrees to port. We will take a look."

Kesseler nodded and repeated the order to the helmsman. The head of the *Rhineland* came round fractionally as the men on the bridge stared out into the rainy darkness. Muller began to pull on his oilskin coat, while Schreiber moved back to the door of the radio room. Weber joined the Captain.

The radio officer sensed their presence and took off his headphones. He held them out so that they could hear the weak voice almost lost in a crackle of interference.

"I still can't get his position," the operator said in exasperation. "It is not a powerful transmitter and he does not seem to know how to use it properly. All that I can understand is the distress signal. He does not seem to hear me at all."

"Keep listening," Schreiber said. "The radar only shows one small boat in this area so we are investigating."

The radio operator nodded and adjusted his headphones again.

Schreiber went back to the radar screen. The blip was now closer. He checked their course and counselled Kesseler and the helmsman to keep the ship steady. Then he moved aside and motioned Weber to join him.

"Herr Weber," he said quietly, "do you think that this incident can be in any way connected with your own presence aboard my ship?"

Weber weighed the question carefully but then shook his head. "No, Captain,

I don't see how there can be any connection." He paused and then added, "Is it so unusual to get a distress call?"

"It is not routine," Schreiber said thoughtfully. "And with you on board I have been expecting some break in the routine."

He shrugged then as though dismissing the idea and began to pull on his oilskins. Weber followed his example and they both collected night glasses before joining Muller who had preceded them out on to the open wing of the bridge.

The rain lashed down, hurled by a thirty-five mile-per-hour wind that was not quite gale force. Ahead the driving bows of the *Rhineland* split asunder the booming seas that ran in heavy black waves from south to east. The ship lurched steadily from starboard to port and then back again. The movement was not enough to bother Schreiber or Muller, but it made Eric Weber feel decidedly off balance. He raised his glasses but saw nothing but more heaving black seas.

After ten minutes Muller suddenly dropped one hand from his glasses, pointed and said sharply; "There!"

Weber saw nothing, but after another three seconds Schreiber dropped his glasses against his chest and moved to the wheel-house door.

"Herr Kesseler, order half engines. Then hard to port."

Kesseler gave the orders. The ship responded and began to wallow more heavily as she lost speed and turned away from the wind. Weber was still straining his eyes through the night glasses, but it was another minute before he saw what the First Officer and the Captain had already seen, the lights of a small boat blinking intermittently through the black squalls of rain. The lights were now dead ahead, and as the distance narrowed he gradually made out the shape of a fishing boat that appeared to be bobbing helplessly on the waves.

"Stop engines!" Schreiber commanded. "Hard to starboard and hold her bows into the wind!"

Again the ship responded. The beat of the engines faded, but while the ship was still under way Kesseler added his weight to that of the helmsman to bring the wheel round. The *Rhineland* swung her bows in a slow half circle into the teeth of the wind and then came to a stop as the long-running waves tried to push her back.

The fishing boat was now only three hundred yards off on their port side. Weber trained his glasses on to the boat's deck and saw two figures hanging on to the wheelhouse and waving frantically. They looked like a man and a boy and the man was pointing towards the stern of the craft where the engine would be housed. The boat balanced on a wave and then slid out of control into a black valley. Then it was lifted again. The man and the boy had their mouths open as though they were shouting hoarsely, but their voices were lost in the wind and rain.

"They have engine trouble," Muller decided.

"Probably broken down, or run out of fuel," Schreiber agreed. "They are drifting and eventually these seas will wreck them on the coast. We will lower the port lifeboat and bring the crew on board. Herr Muller, you will take charge of the boat."

★ ★ ★

In the cramped wheelhouse of the *Beatriz* Hasan Bakarat watched the lifeboat as it was lowered slowly down the steel flank of the freighter's hull. The boat vanished from his sight as it reached sea level but he was confident that it was on its way. He was crouching low, with his Schmeisser machine pistol gripped firmly in his right hand. His left hand gripped the steadying handrail that ran around the inside of the wheel-house and his arm ached with the effort of bracing himself against the violent rolling and tossing of the boat. Behind him crouched Takaaki and Hayashi. They were keeping their heads low because they knew that there would be men with binoculars on the *Rhineland*'s bridge.

Bakarat was cursing the rough weather which was a definite disadvantage now that they had stopped the engine to leave the *Beatriz* at the mercy of the heavy seas. The rain and the darkness made excellent cover, but the wind and the waves that towered over the small craft he could have done without. Already Jiro Yotaro had been helplessly sick, and he wondered how the others were feeling confined with the retching Yotaro in the diesel and fish polluted prison below decks.

They waited while the *Beatriz* lifted and plunged, flung from wave to wave like a puppet ship with broken strings. Now that the *Rhineland* had answered their call there was no further need to man the radio. There was nothing to do now but bear with their position until the lifeboat arrived.

On the deck of the *Beatriz* Giovanni Vasquez and his son were soaked to the skin, their throats were raw with shouting and their bodies cowed by the battering of wind and rain. Standing upright they saw the *Rhineland*'s lifeboat struggling to reach them and weakly they continued to wave. They were still ignorant of what was happening and why, and in their fear and confusion they could only obey the orders they had been given. Vasquez no longer cared for himself or his boat but hoped that his blind obedience might save his son. The approaching lifeboat became a symbol of hope that could not have been more real if the *Beatriz* had been in genuine danger of sinking, for to Vasquez it promised some kind of release from his ordeal.

The lifeboat came alongside. A rope was hurled by one of the German seamen and Vasquez caught it and made it fast. Muller shouted at the boy now standing by helplessly while his father secured the rope. The language barrier was between them and Luis could only stare back dumbly. The two boats rose and fell together as Vasquez straightened up and indicated that the rope was tied. The German seamen began to haul on the line and the lifeboat and the fishing boat closed together. The wind howled, rain slashed across the two craft, and Muller balanced in the bows ready to jump the narrowing gap.

In that moment Takaaki and Hayashi burst out of the wheel-house with wild shrieks of triumph. The samurai swords swung naked in their hands and with powerful, full-swing blows they neatly decapitated both Vasquez and his son where they stood.

Muller stared in horror. He saw the two heads rolling along the wet deck towards the bows of the fishing boat. Then the two bodies seemed to sag and collapse to reveal the two grinning Japanese with the long, red-stained swords.

On his first trip to sea Muller had been a boy Lieutenant in a U-boat. He had seen blood and death and horror before and he had learned to react to it. He reacted now and the move cost him his life. He grabbed at the hand axe that was standard equipment in the bows of all lifeboats and tried to wrench it free from its retaining clips. He succeeded but then Bakarat stepped between the two Japanese and shot him dead with a short burst of gunfire from his machine pistol.

★ ★ ★

Eric Weber had no part to play in the rescue operation, but he had remained on the bridge beside Schreiber, watching through the powerful night glasses. They both witnessed the events on board the fishing boat.

"Meine Gott," Schreiber said aghast.

"There's a gun in my cabin," Weber said briefly. "I'll get it."

He turned to the back of the bridge

75

and ran down the companionway to the deck below. The gun was a Walther 0.38 automatic that was locked in the drawer beside his bunk. He didn't know what use it could be in this situation but he did know that he wanted it in his hand. He reached the deck and turned towards his cabin, but then a foot kicked out from the dark patch of shadow beneath the companionway. Weber tripped and crashed in a headlong dive across the wet deck. The force of his own momentum carried him skidding into the scuppers where he came to rest with his shoulder bruised and his brain reeling.

Figures loomed over him, four of them, blurred and threatening in the rain and darkness. Even so Weber recognized the group of four Arab deckhands who formed part of the ship's crew. He knew then that the Walther might as well be a million miles away, for the Arabs all carried Schmeisser machine pistols.

"Jabril, lift him up and bring him to the bridge."

Weber knew that the man who gave the order was named Zakaria, and that he was the leader of this particular group. The man named Jabril dragged the still dazed Weber to his feet while Zakaria and the other two ran to the bridge.

Schreiber and Kesseler faced the sudden invasion of the three men with machine pistols. They froze, but then Schreiber recognized the faces from his crew and his own features mottled with fury.

"The *Rhineland* is now under the command of Palestine Liberation Forces," Zakaria told him curtly. "You will obey my orders until our friends return with your boat."

"No!" Schreiber roared. "I am the Captain of this ship and you will give that weapon to me."

He marched forward with his shoulders back and his eyes blazing beneath the gold of his cap. These men were rabble

77

from the crew's mess deck and he relied upon his own unquestionable authority to continue his mastery of the ship and its destiny. Zakaria looked momentarily astonished and the men on either side of him fell back. Kesseler took courage and advanced to support the Captain. Schreiber reached out a bear-like hand to tear the machine pistol aside, and then Zakaria recovered his composure and squeezed the trigger.

Schreiber's face registered shock and then amazement. Not for one moment had he expected to die, for at sea he was God aboard the *Rhineland* and was not in the nature of Gods to contemplate their own downfall. The crash of bullets drove him backwards and then he fell dead at Kesseler's feet.

The Second Officer stopped in mid-stride, and for a moment his face was an exact mirror of the Captain's. Then he slowly raised his hands above his head.

Eric Weber stumbled on to the

bridge with Jabril's machine pistol jabbing against his spine and he too lifted his hands.

Zakaria was now smiling with satisfaction.

# 5

THERE was a long silence on the bridge of the *Rhineland*. Kesseler, the helmsman and the two seamen on the duty watch were struck dumb, staring down with frozen tongues in tight mouths set in white faces. The lifeless body of the Captain bled without sound. Zakaria and his three companions from the lower decks held undisputed command and for the moment they saw no more need for words. They simply waited for their friends to join them.

Eric Weber stared from Schreiber to the faces of the four Arabs and the muzzles of the four machine pistols and he felt anger and a sense of guilt boiling within his chest. He felt anger at the senseless butchery and guilt because he had failed. For four months he had sailed back and forth on the *Rhineland*

and now when the moment had come he had proved hopelessly incompetent. Somehow the four men he had been set to watch had smuggled their weapons aboard under his very nose, and that alone was something that should never have happened.

Weber realized bitterly that he had never taken this threat seriously enough, even though he should have known that the threat was real. Schreiber had felt a moment of doubt after he had changed course, but even then Weber had failed to see any possibility of a connection between the distressed fishing boat and his own presence aboard the *Rhineland*. The Captain had spelled the danger out for him, but still his imagination had been too small to foresee what was to come. It was obvious now that he should have checked on the whereabouts of the four Arab deckhands the moment he knew that an unscheduled event was taking place. The first trouble-free voyage had lulled him into a sense of complacency with the conviction that he was wasting his time, but that was no excuse. At the very least he should be lying dead with the Walther 0.38 in his hand. Instead it was the unarmed Captain and Muller who had died trying to hold their ship. He was alive but helpless, and the Walther still lay useless and unfired in the drawer beside his bunk. The magnitude of his mistakes and the bloody consequences appalled him.

Slowly Weber became aware that although every man on the bridge was silent there was still sound. The wind still roared and the rain still lashed down on the superstructure. The heavy seas still crashed over the bows and now the *Rhineland* was swinging slowly to port. She began to roll more heavily.

Kesseler felt the motion and with it the realization that he was the only effective deck officer left alive. He looked from the Captain to the helmsman and found his voice.

"Hold that wheel steady — three

degrees to starboard and keep her into the wind."

Kesseler's voice was hoarse. The helmsman was incapable of answering but he remembered his job and obeyed.

Weber accepted that even when death and disaster struck life went on. His mistakes were multiple but they were all in the past. Dwelling on what had already happened and what he should have done to prevent it was all a waste of time. The past was unalterable and the dead beyond resurrection. He took the first step to controlling his emotions, crushing down the feelings of guilt and failure, and deciding that now he must wipe his mind clean and think only of the present and the future. From this point on he could afford no more mistakes. He looked into the dark, pockmarked face of Zakaria as though for the first time, searching for a trace of weakness.

Zakaria stared back at him curiously, wondering what this shocked blonde fool was thinking. Something in the grim blue eyes caused him a moment of unease, but then he decided that it was not important. He moved forward and stooped over the dead body of the Captain. Casually he reached for the night glasses that still lay on Schreiber's chest. He pulled them free, dislodging the gold-peaked cap as he tugged the strap from behind the dead man's neck. He slung his machine pistol over one shoulder and pulled out a grubby handkerchief to wipe the blood spots from the lens of the binoculars.

Kesseler looked ready to commit suicide as he watched this act of careless violation. There were three machine pistols still levelled and Weber shook his head in a warning sign. The Second Officer clenched his fists and the sweat trickled down the side of his face. Zakaria ignored them and went out on to the wing of the bridge to look through the binoculars.

He came back quickly, wet with rain.

"They have scuttled the fishing boat," he told his companions. "And the lifeboat is returning." He looked to Kesseler and unslung his machine pistol again. "You are the senior officer now. Give the orders for the boat to be hoisted back on board."

Kesseler hesitated, but there were loyal crewmen in the boat and defiance would serve no purpose. He said bitterly:

"Herr Weber, go to the boatdeck and take charge."

Weber saw no immediate alternative and nodded slowly. He left the bridge and two of the armed Arabs followed at his heels. The team of sailors who had lowered the lifeboat were still waiting by the winches. They had heard the gunfire, both from the bridge and from the fishing boat, and now their faces registered various expressions from bafflement to dismay as they saw the two machine pistols at Weber's back. They asked questions but the man named Jabril curtly told them

85

to be quiet. Weber warned them that the Captain was already dead and they obeyed.

Fortunately the sailors knew their own job and so Weber's total inexperience in raising and lowering lifeboats was hardly noticeable. The lifeboat came alongside and after some initial difficulty caused by the rough sea the German crewmen on board succeeded in hooking on to the blocks and lines swinging dangerously from the *Rhineland*'s davits. Weber gave the order and the electric motors were started to winch the lifeboat back into its place on the boatdeck.

Hasan Bakarat was the first man to step down on to the freighter's deck, smiling and holding his machine pistol at the ready. Jabril welcomed him warmly as Takaaki and the other members of the combined groups joined them. Yotaro was green with sea-sickness and had to be helped aboard, and Farraj now had charge of the essential suitcase.

The reunion on the boatdeck was brief and then Bakarat ordered Weber to precede them all back to the bridge. There the reunion was continued with Bakarat and Zakaria falling into each other's arms and laughing with delight. With beaming faces the two groups congratulated each other. Then Bakarat became serious, he stood back and said gravely.

"No justice for Palestine — "

" — No peace for the world!"

Zakaria concluded the phrase and briefly their smiles returned. He looked around the faces of his new-found friends and then a hint of uncertainty betrayed itself in his eyes.

"Hasan, it is good to see you all again. It has been so long since we last met in Paris. But one face is missing — where is our friend Hamani?"

"Hamani is dead," Bakarat told him. "Somehow the *Shinbeth* picked up his trail in Rome. They murdered him. The rest of us had to leave for Madrid earlier than we planned, but otherwise

Hamani's death has not interferred with our operation."

"Hamani dead!" Zakaria repeated. Then he cursed, "May Allah put the blight of death upon all Jews. May the plague rot all Israel!"

"Enough." Takaaki stepped forward. The Japanese was smaller in stature than the two Arabs but in addition to the machine pistol in his hands the hilt of his samurai sword thrust up behind his left shoulder and his eyes were black flint behind his spectacles. "This ship must get under way," he continued. "There is not much time. We must intercept in three hours."

"You are right," Bakarat agreed. He looked down at the dead body on the deck for the first time, recognizing the four golden shoulder bars. "It is a pity you killed the Captain," he told Zakaria. "Especially as I had to kill the First Officer."

"The Second Officer is alive," Zakaria said carelessly.

Bakarat allowed himself a smile and

then looked at Kesseler. "You will have to do — get this ship under way and then we will plot your new course."

Kesseler clamped his jaws together hard. He wanted to refuse, but there was no sense in letting the *Rhineland* simply drift to eventual destruction on the rocks of the Spanish coast. He finally turned to the engine room telegraph and pulled the lever over to signal full ahead.

The *Rhineland* gave a lurch a few seconds later as the engines began to turn, and then her bows started to push forward into the gathering storm.

Eric Weber risked one question: "You went to a lot of trouble to capture this ship. You must have planned for months and you've killed four men. Why?"

Takaaki looked at him disdainfully. Zakaria and the others smiled. Then Bakarat gave him an oblique answer.

"The English have a saying that it takes a sprat to catch a mackerel. Well, my friend, the *Beatriz* was our sprat and the *Rhineland* is our mackerel — and now we shall use our mackerel to catch a whale!"

★ ★ ★

Earlier that evening, while it was still six o'clock in Rome, Roberto Gaiani had knocked on the door of a fifth floor apartment that was only ten minutes away from Bakarat's old domicile in the Via Ventura. Victor Bardini was at Gaiani's side and after a few moments the door was opened by an attractive but somewhat brazen looking young woman in a white blouse and a dark skirt. She stared blankly at the two strangers.

"Miss Sonia Rocco?" Gaiani showed her his identification card as he spoke. "We would like to talk to you if it is convenient."

He entered the room, giving her no real opportunity to argue. Behind him Bardini closed the door. Sonia Rocco looked startled and a little afraid.

"I haven't done anything — what do you want?"

Gaiani wondered wearily whether any suspect would ever surprise him with an original response. However, he smiled at her and gestured to a chair.

"Let us both sit down, then I will tell you."

Hesitantly Sonia complied, making an effort not to show too much cleavage or thigh. Bardini sensed her embarrassment and moved away as though absent-mindedly examining the room. Gaiani pulled up another chair and faced her. He was a family man with three daughters of his own, so now he pretended that this was his own Lucia who was in trouble. It helped him to set a more gentle atmosphere which he hoped would encourage the girl to talk.

"It is about a friend of yours, an Algerian named Hasan Bakarat. He is missing from his apartment and I hope that you may be able to help us to find him."

Sonia's throat was suddenly dry. She had worried about Hasan for the past week, knowing only that he must be in some kind of trouble. Now the arrival of these two policemen confirmed her fears. She did not know whether Hasan was a criminal or not, although she suspected that he probably was, but she did know that he had no love for the police. He had told her to wait and say nothing until he came to her, and her first thought was to wonder how he would want her to act now. Instinctively she decided that he would want her to say nothing.

"I don't know any man of that name, Inspector," she said slowly. "I think you must have made a mistake."

"Perhaps you only knew him by a nickname." Gaiani said helpfully. "Or perhaps he gave you a false name. But you did visit him regularly at an apartment in building number twenty-five on the Via Ventura. The apartment number was B-3."

Sonia swallowed hard and looked

down at her knees. "That means nothing to me. It is still all a mistake."

"Hasan Bakarat was your lover for the past six months," Gaiani said carefully. "The caretaker at the apartment block on the Via Ventura is an observant and reasonably intelligent woman. She has noticed that you have visited Bakarat at least two or three times a week, and that you often stayed overnight. She does not know your name or where you live, but she has noticed that on two or three occasions you wore a pale green overall — the type that a shopgirl might wear. Consequently my Sergeant has accompanied the caretaker on a long tour, one that started with the shops in the immediate radius of the Via Ventura and then gradually expanded outwards. It is a pity that you work so far from your home, for it has taken us four days to find the right shop."

He smiled sadly. "There is a little flower shop near to the Piazza di

Spagna, where the girls who sell the flowers are all pretty and they all wear pale green overall coats. The caretaker identified you, and your employer gave Sergeant Bardini your name and address. I decided that we would interview you here in your own home. You see, we want you to help us — we have no desire to embarrass you."

"It is still a mistake," Sonia persisted desperately. She could think of nothing else to say.

"The woman who was Bakarat's mistress left her fingerprints all over his apartment," Gaiani informed her. "If you insist I can have your fingerprints taken for comparison. That will be messy, and I think a waste of time, but it will conclusively determine the argument. Is it necessary?"

Sonia saw that she was trapped. She bit her lip and shook her head.

"Then tell me about this man Bakarat."

"There is nothing to tell. He was

just a friend — a lover, if you must know all."

"Then why did you make such efforts to deny him?" Gaiani spread his hands and looked baffled. "It is not so wrong for a young girl to have a lover — or is there something about him that the police should not know?"

"No — why should there be?"

"Why should you pretend that you did not know him?"

Sonia stared at him and did not answer.

"Do you know where your friend is now?"

"I only know that he has left Rome."

"He took a plane to Madrid," Gaiani informed her. "Perhaps he has abandoned you?"

"No."

"Did you know that he had gone to Madrid?"

"No."

"Then how do you know that he has not abandoned you?"

"I know. He will come back."

"If he loves you enough to come back to Rome, then perhaps he loved you enough to share his plans," Gaiani suggested. "What were his plans?"

"I don't know. Hasan never told me."

"But he was your lover for six months," Gaiani repeated. "You shared his bed. You must have talked. And even if he did not explain anything of his future intentions you must have formed some ideas of your own. You must have met his friends — you would overhear things."

"No." Sonia felt as though desperation was strangling the words in her throat, as though any admission would be a betrayal of Hasan. "His friends never called while I was there. He never talked of any plans."

"You are not being helpful," Gaiani protested. "Do you really expect me to believe that you knew this man for six months, and yet at the same time you knew nothing about him."

"His name was Hasan," Sonia said.

"He came from Algeria and he was looking for work." She felt as though even that was saying too much.

Gaiani stared at her shrewdly. She was cracking and under pressure she would break, but at the same time he doubted whether Hasan Bakarat would have been fool enough to have told her anything of importance. Unfortunately she was the only possible lead that he had, and instinct told him that it was imperative that he should discover what Bakarat and his companions had plotted during their stay in Rome. The only way was to break her quickly and then squeeze every shred of memory out of her subconscious mind in the hope that something of value would emerge. He decided to show her a photograph of the dead man Hamani in the hope that it might shock her into defeat.

Sonia watched his left hand dip inside his coat. She didn't know what he intended but suddenly her impulse was to run. Her love for Bakarat was a blind thing built on foundations of twisted emotion, at core it consisted of unquestioning devotion. She knew in her heart that he had planned some great crime, but she also knew that it was not for profit but for a cause. She had sensed the fierce anger and frustration that could now find its outlets only in violence and in hate, and somehow she knew that he was as much a victim as a predator. That was why she had loved him and accepted his frequent cruelty. She had to love and help him because he could not love or help himself. His destiny was ordained by race and birth, and now it was only important that she did not betray him.

In that she did not trust herself, for she knew that she was weak and that despite his deceptively friendly smile the man before her was sharp and strong. So she ran, in the moment that Gaiani's hand was withdrawing his wallet she jumped up and dashed past him on his left side.

Gaiani was fast but with his hand caught momentarily inside his own coat he was at a disadvantage. Sonia was at the door as he sprang up to chase her and Bardini was racing over from the far side of the room. Sonia slipped through the door and slammed it behind her as she ran for the top of the stairs. The door was whipped open almost instantaneously and Gaiani shouted. Sonia saw the head and shoulders of a bull-like policeman in uniform charging up the stairs to meet her and in panic she fled past the top of the staircase and along the narrow corridor. At the far end was a glass panelled door that opened on to a steel fire escape.

Sonia heard the three men pounding behind her. Terror gripped her and even as she ran she knew that escape was impossible. Then one of her high heels caught in a wrinkle in the carpet and threw her forward. She screamed as her body crashed through the glass door, and then she hit the steel platform of the fire escape outside. There was no way that she could stop her forward dive and she was still screaming as she skidded off the platform, passing beneath the safety rail and flailing out into space. This was the fifth floor and after five seconds the long scream stopped.

Gaiani's last link with Hasan Bakarat was gone.

# 6

TWENTY-FIVE miles off the coast of Spain the *Monolith* carved a relentless path through the Atlantic seas like some gigantic dinosaur of the deep. More than a thousand feet from bow to stern her vast green-painted deck provided enough space to land a flight of aircraft if the clutter of pipelines, valve wheels and pump couplings had been cleared away. The white island superstructure at the stern of the ship rose a sheer seventy feet above the deck, topped by the radio mast and radar scanner, and yet the whole was dwarfed by the overall length of the hull. The supertanker was a 250,000 ton monster, and the volatile nature of her cargo meant that she carried a thermal energy potential equal to that of a nuclear warhead.

It was four and a half weeks since

the *Monolith* had taken on board a full cargo of crude oil from the sun-blistered rock island of Kharg in the Persian Gulf. She had ploughed stolidly south through the Indian Ocean, with the oil rumbling low in her belly as the gentle motion rolled it back and forth through the deep vents in the huge storage tanks. She had rounded the Cape of Good Hope and turned north. Now the long hot days and balmy nights of the tropics were far behind, so far the voyage had been uneventful and she was on the last lap home. Her destination was the great Europort oil terminal at Rotterdam.

In the saloon a party was in progress. The ship's company included five wives and six children, the focus of the sometimes desperate social life which helped to make the monotony of tanker existence bearable. Any birthday at sea was sufficient cause for a celebration, and a birthday party for one of the children was generally heralded with a three-day fanfare of preparations.

Today was the birthday of the twins, Jackie Spencer's two little daughters, Gillian and Julie, were four years old, and this double event was greeted with as much enthusiasm as a royal wedding. The cooks had excelled themselves, and it had already been remarked that any other ship but the *Monolith* would have sunk beneath the mountains of cakes, trifles and jellies that had been proudly produced from the galley. The saloon was hung with *happy birthday* streamers and a multitude of balloons, and the noise was a combination of bangs, laughter, music and squealing excitement.

Bruce Fraser paused in the doorway to watch. The Chief Officer of the *Monolith* had keen grey eyes in a square, sun-tanned face. His shoulders were broad, carrying the authority of his three gold bars with ease. When he smiled his rugged features seemed to lose a few of his forty-three years and the lively antics of the children made it impossible to hold back a smile.

The present game was musical chairs, played by the five eldest children, three of the wives and all the available junior officers. Don Campbell, the ginger-headed Second Engineer and father of the two boys who were making the most noise, was playing cheerfully at the piano. Philip Eldridge, the ship's tall and boyishly handsome Third Officer was in charge of taking away the chairs with each break in the music, and naturally it was the adults who were the first to fall out.

Elizabeth Fergusson, the wife of the dour and formidable Chief Engineer appeared abruptly at Frazer's side. Her grey hair had been freshly permed and set for the occasion and at fifty-nine there was still a twinkle in her eye. The Captain was a bachelor and Fraser had lost his wife in a tragic road accident three years before. That made Elizabeth the undisputed senior lady of the ship.

"Mister Fraser, you are improperly dressed," she informed him. She removed his peaked cap and hung it neatly on a peg, replacing it with a crown of red crepe paper.

"Remind me to take it off before I return to the bridge," Fraser said.

"Fiddlesticks to the bridge, our party is much more important. Why isn't the Captain here?"

"Somebody has to point the ship in the right direction."

"A likely story," She smiled at him confidentially. "The trouble with dear Hugh is that he's afraid of women."

"Captain Armstrong simply understands that ships are easier to handle," Fraser assured her. Then he changed the subject. "How is the party going?"

"Splendidly. Stephen and Angus have had two fights. Ian and Gillian have both been sick. The carpets and the tablecloths are ruined, and the baby has only cried once. It couldn't be better."

Fraser laughed and led her over to the bar. The children would eventually be put to bed blissfully exhausted and the adults would continue the party far into the night. Some mild drinking had already started and Fraser ordered a small whisky.

Jackie Spencer and Jane Campbell approached together, having both been squeezed out of the musical chairs game. They were both flushed and breathless. Jackie was dark and slim and Jane blonde and slightly plump.

"I wouldn't have believed that any two women could be directly responsible for all this commotion," Fraser joked.

Jackie was the mother of five-year old Stephen as well as the twin girls, while Jane was the mother of four-year old Angus and three-year old Ian.

"Our children are only making half the noise," Jackie protested. "It's the officers who are making the rest."

They drank two quick sherries and returned to the fray as the musical chairs game ended. The red-headed Angus had been declared the winner and another game had to be organized quickly to console the losers. A balloon burst with a bang, Julie was shouting because someone had trampled on her party hat and Ian was in danger of losing his trousers. Elizabeth moved to help restore order, for she commanded the saloon as effectively as her husband commanded the engine room or the Captain the bridge.

Fraser was alone and wandered over to talk to Mary Darling, the youngest of the five wives. Mary was barely twenty, with rich honey-blonde hair and bright blue eyes. She was also the quietest and shyest of the group and was often embarrassed by her own name. She was married to the ship's Third Engineer and carried their eleven month baby in her arms.

"He's a bonny bairn," Fraser told her. "And I do believe he gets bonnier every day."

Mary looked up at him, smiling and blushing at the same time.

"He can sleep through this," she said. "But tonight when he should be sleeping he'll make more noise than all of them."

"You should let George take him down into the engine room. There he won't disturb anybody."

"It's hot and dirty down there — but you could have him on the bridge."

"Now that would upset the Captain."

They talked for a while and then Mary decided that she would take the baby to her cabin in the hope that he would continue sleeping. After she had gone Fraser sipped his whisky and idly watched the rest of the festivities.

His gaze rested briefly on Sue Deverell, the wife of the Second Officer, and the suggestion of a frown reached the corners of his mouth. Sue was by far the most attractive woman on board and with her superb figure always shown off to its best advantage, her easy laughter and her eyes always teasing, she was becoming something of a shipboard problem. Apart from Elizabeth, whose sons were now grown up and had gone their own way, she was the only woman with no children. That meant extra time on her hands and because of her flirtatious nature the younger unmarried officers tended to flock around her. She had the ability to encourage their attentions without being blatant, and although it would be difficult for her to be unfaithful in such a closely confined community, Fraser knew that recently her husband had been showing signs of acute jealously.

John Deverell was at that moment standing watch on the bridge with the Captain and so Sue was free to be chatted keenly by Derek Holbrook, the Third Radio Officer. Holbrook was a junior just finding his feet and Sue was obviously amused by the wistful hope in his eyes. At the same time Philip Eldridge who usually led her field of courtiers was risking a series of dark, sidelong glances.

Fraser decided that the issue was best left ignored. It was too delicate an area for the heavy hand of authority. He turned his head and watched the

Second Radio Officer strumming his guitar.

Anthony Gaye had slender, sensitive fingers and a fine, gentle voice. He played and sang well and the children became almost quiet for a few minutes as they listened to his rendering of the magic dragon . . . .

Fraser reflected that at least he didn't have to worry about Anthony Gaye sticking his neck out in the same direction as Holbrook and Eldridge, for Gaye was cheerfully and unapologetically homosexual.

At five minutes to twelve Fraser ascended to the bridge to take over the midnight watch. Eldridge and Gaye accompanied him. By that time the children had all been carried sleepily away and the women had returned to transform the party into a dance. Campbell was still playing the piano and Holbrook, although less accomplished, had taken over Gaye's guitar.

Captain Hugh Armstrong, the master

of the *Monolith*, greeted them formally and handed command to Fraser with the usual accurate breakdown of information regarding their present position, speed and course. He was a tall man of sixty with fierce, bushy eyebrows beneath the weight of gold braid on the peak of his cap. He had the reputation of being an unemotional martinet, but in fact he ruled his huge, sea-borne household rather like a Victorian father. He had an affection for most of the lives that were his responsibility which he would never exhibit.

Eight bells rang. The new helmsman and lookouts appeared and the changeover was complete. Gaye took over the radio room from Alan Spencer, the departing Chief Radio Officer. Eldridge took up a position by the radar scanner vacated by John Deverell and awkwardly bid the Second Officer goodnight. Eldridge had spent the last ten minutes dancing with Sue.

The Captain paused for a final word with his Chief Officer.

"How is the party going?"

"They're having fun," Fraser told him. "Elizabeth swears you won't dare show your face."

Armstrong smiled. Elizabeth Fergusson knew him well but loyally kept his secret by pretending to believe in his self-projected image.

"That leaves me no choice," he said. "I have to go."

Armstrong left the bridge.

Fraser smiled at the Captain's feigned reluctance and then he spent the next few minutes in studying the chart. He double-checked their course and speed and calculated that in approximately four hours they would be rounding Cape Finisterre. There were no problems and so he moved forward to look down through the bridge window on to the long deck far below. The black seas beyond were building up in height and it was beginning to rain. The latest weather forecast gave a gale warning for the Bay of Biscay, but for the moment the winds were only force five, building up to six. The giant bulk of the *Monolith* rolled slowly, her sheer size making her almost disdainful of the threatening elements.

The men on the bridge relaxed into boredom. The midnight watch was the dead watch, the longest four hours out of every day. It was a time for thinking and each man was alone with his thoughts. Fraser thought of Moira, now a fond memory from another time; he could still picture the laughing faces of the children at the party, and he wished that they had had children of their own.

The night hours crawled by.

"Mister Fraser!"

The time was two twenty-five a.m. and the Third Officer's voice was calm. Fraser joined him by the twin radar screens. One radar kept a close vigil over a six mile radius around the ship, while the other ranged up to twenty-four miles ahead. The long range screen had picked up a blip on the outer perimeter of its sweep.

"She's north-north-east of our position, steaming southwest-by-west," Eldridge said quietly. "On her present course she must cross our path."

Fraser stared down at the green glow of the screen, frowning at the brighter spot of light that marked the position of the unknown vessel. Now the audio signal was also sounding clear, a distinct ping each time the moving radial line swept over the bright spot.

"The size of the blip indicates a ship of about ten thousand tons," Fraser mused. "The average vessel of that weight makes about fifteen knots." He did some rapid mental calculations and finished, "If she holds her present course at that estimated speed we will collide in forty-five minutes."

"So we have to change course," Eldridge said.

"Not yet, Philip. Remember that we will also be registering on the radar screen of that other ship. The smallest vessel has the greatest manoeuvrability, so we'll give them time to wake up and take the necessary avoiding action."

They waited five minutes.

"She must be an old ship with obsolete equipment," Eldridge guessed. "Her radar must have a limited range."

Fraser was mentally re-assessing the situation and weighing his options. He could reduce speed and let the mystery ship pass in front of them, or he could order a change of course. With the latter he had two choices, port or starboard, and if the men on the bridge of the other ship picked up the *Monolith* on their screen and made a hasty change of direction in the same moment then they could still collide. The thinking time was narrowing for both ships, but Fraser waited for another five minutes before making his decision.

"You were right the first time," he told Eldridge.

Then he moved over to the telephone and called the Captain's suite. Armstrong answered promptly.

"Fraser here, sir. Sorry to disturb you but we're on a collision course with another vessel. I'm proposing to change course."

"Thank you, Mister Fraser." From Armstrong's voice it was impossible to tell that he had been abruptly woken from his sleep. He continued evenly, "I'll attend on the bridge."

Fraser went back to the radar screens and waited until Armstrong appeared. The blip that represented the unknown ship was still approaching on the same course and at the same speed. Now it was only sixteen miles away and the accompanying ping, ping, ping, was growing louder.

"Our course, speed and position, Mister Fraser?" Armstrong said briefly.

Fraser told him.

"And you propose?"

"A twenty degree course change to starboard, sir."

"That will turn us towards the coast — and if that ship ahead has either Vigo or Lisbon as her destination then she will also turn to follow the coast."

"She's well round the Cape, sir, and she's been maintaining her present course since she was first picked up on the radar. If she was intending to turn then I think she would have made that turn by now. My feeling is that she's set on south-west-by-west, and if we carry on or turn to port then either way we stay on a collision course."

Armstrong smiled. "Very well, Mister Fraser. I approve your decision."

Fraser hoped that he was right. He turned to the helmsman at the wheel and said briskly:

"Hard to starboard, twenty degrees!"

The helmsman obeyed. Slowly, ponderously, with infinite reluctance the great weight of the *Monolith* began to swing round. The rain that was now driving down shifted to the port windows of the bridge where it seemed to hammer more loudly than before. The world was one of pitch darkness beyond the range of the tanker's lights, and the two radar screens were her only eyes. The distant bows lifted and the long hull heaved and tilted as she settled into her new course.

Two minutes later Eldridge spoke sharply beside the radar screens.

"Sir, the other ship has changed course towards us. We're on a collision course again."

Fraser and Armstrong came closer.

"Damn her," Fraser said. "They must have spotted us just before we made the turn — so now they've turned right into us."

"Slow engines!" Armstrong called, and the nearest seaman promptly rang down the order on the engine room telegraph.

When the jangle of the telegraph died away there was silence except for the steady bleeping of the audio signal from the radar. Fraser and Armstrong watched the corresponding speck of light flashing on the screen with frustration. They were both hoping that the other Captain would quickly realize what had happened and correct his mistake, knowing that if the two ships again made simultaneous corrections then the result could be fatal. They were playing a blind game of chess with limited moves, and another false move could zigzag them to disaster.

The stranger showed no indication of making another change of course. The two vessels were now only twelve miles apart and still on a collision course.

Armstrong turned to his Third Officer.

"Mister Eldridge, give my compliments to the Radio Officer and ask him to contact that ship."

"Aye, aye, sir," Eldridge moved to obey.

Armstrong glanced at Fraser. "We'll maintain this course and reduced speed for five minutes," he decided. "Then if they haven't made a move and we haven't raised them on the radio we'll resume our original course."

Fraser nodded. "To move, or not to move," he misquoted wryly.

Armstrong cracked a bleak smile.

At that moment Anthony Gaye appeared from the radio room, intercepting Eldridge at the door. The Second Radio Officer looked unusually serious and handed Eldridge a message sheet. Eldridge brought it quickly to the radar screens.

"We're picking up a distress call," he told the Captain and Chief Officer together. "It's coming from that ship dead ahead."

# 7

ARMSTRONG stared down at the single sheet torn from the radio message pad. "Is this all?" he demanded.

Eldridge nodded. "For the moment, sir. Mister Gaye is trying to get more details."

Armstrong handed the sheet to Fraser. "Just a blunt *mayday* call. The ship hasn't identified itself or given its position — but it's close and immediately ahead of us."

Fraser stared down at the radar screen. "She's about eleven miles away and there's nothing else within our area."

Armstrong turned to one of the seamen attending on the bridge. "Yates, go to the radio room and act as messenger for Mister Gaye. I want any further information relayed as soon as it arrives."

"Aye, aye, sir!" Yates moved smartly to obey.

There was silence on the bridge again except for the monotonous *pinging* from the radar screen. The three men watched and waited while the minutes ticked away.

"She's stopped," Eldridge said suddenly.

The blip of light that had been edging slowly towards the centre of the screen had stopped moving. Now it was simply registering in one position.

"Distance about nine miles," Fraser said quietly.

He looked to Armstrong and waited. They both knew that an emergency stop for the *Monolith* was no routine measure to be undertaken lightly. Normally the order for propeller speed to decrease would be given at least two hours and twenty miles before the ship was due to reach port. Their 250,000 ton monster needed sea room and time to make any manoeuvre. A full stop in anything less than five miles and twenty-five minutes was impossible, and even then the ship would be slewing sideways out of control.

Yates appeared from the radio room.

"From Mister Gaye, sir. The ship ahead is still sending out a continuous distress call, but there's no further information. Mister Gaye keeps asking them to state their position and the situation on board, but they don't appear to be receiving him."

"Thank you, Yates," Armstrong acknowledged. "Tell Mister Gaye to keep trying."

Yates nodded and hurried back to the radio room.

Eldridge looked anxious as he stared down at the radar screen. "It has to be that ship," he said. "But what the hell are they playing at?"

"They were maintaining a steady course but now they've lost way," Fraser spelled it out calmly. "Also the man sending out the *mayday* call is obviously not a trained radio officer. Even if their set isn't receiving and they're not picking up our call, only an amateur would neglect to send such basic information as the ship's name and position. My guess is that something happened suddenly, and that the radio operator and her senior deck officers are in some way incapacitated."

Armstrong nodded in agreement. "One possibility is that they're on fire, or that they've suffered an explosion. In any case we can't ignore a distress call and there's only one way to find out."

He moved to the telephone and dialled the Chief Engineer's cabin.

"Mister Ferguson —Captain Armstrong here on the bridge. My apologies to Elizabeth, but I'd like you to take command of the engine room. We've received a *mayday* and I'm ordering an emergency stop."

★ ★ ★

The *Monolith* took six miles and thirty-five minutes to slither to a halt and in the last half mile her stern swung round in a vast, swinging semi-circle that brought her broadside on to her original course. In the final stages the great bulk of the supertanker was hopelessly beyond control, and if she had swung too close to the unknown mystery ship, or to the rocks and shallows of the Spanish coast, then disaster on a colossal scale would have been unavoidable. With the *Monolith* there could be no last minute rectification of mistakes. Captain Hugh Armstrong knew these facts only too well and so he made no mistakes. During the initial part of the operation while control remained he used a lifetime of polished skill, and proved his mastery of his ship and the sea. When the supertanker came to rest the long black Atlantic seas that had been rolling up on her port beam were now dividing squarely on either side of the blunt bows, and the vessel emitting the frantic distress call was only half a mile away.

Fraser stood close to the bridge window with a pair of powerful night glasses held to his eyes. The rain had eased and through the darkness he could clearly make out the lights and outline of a stubby old freighter of about ten thousand tons. He couldn't read the name on her bows but there was a nameboard on the side of the bridge that was lit up by the bridge lights.

"She's the *Rhineland*," Fraser said. "Probably a German." He frowned and added. "I can't see a soul on her bridge and her decks are deserted. Yet she looks normal enough otherwise. There's no sign of fire damage."

Armstrong studied the ship in thoughtful silence.

"Perhaps they've already abandoned her," Eldridge offered.

"There's no reason why they should," Fraser told him.

"The ship is high in the water and she's not showing a list or any other sign of sinking."

"Another *Marie Celeste*," Armstrong said without humour. The *Rhineland* had stopped transmitting her distress call and for the past ten minutes there had been radio silence. The situation was unreal with no ready explanation and Armstrong had no fondness for mysteries that endangered his own command.

"Her port lifeboats are still in position," Fraser observed. "If they have abandoned ship then they took to the starboard boats."

He searched the black seas but saw no trace of a lifeboat.

Armstrong did the same and finally lowered his glasses.

"We'll launch our own starboard lifeboat, Mister Fraser. By now Mister Deverell should have organized the boat crew. You will take command and tell Mister Deverell that once the boat is lowered he is to report back here to me."

Armstrong turned to take note of the remaining officers on his bridge. Alan

Spencer had been recalled along with John Deverell and now the Captain addressed his Chief Radio Officer.

"Mister Spencer, please take over the radio room here on the *Monolith*. I shall want Mister Gaye to accompany Mister Fraser and man the emergency transmitter in the lifeboat. I want to be in constant radio contact. Mister Eldridge, you will also accompany Mister Fraser."

There were nods of assent. Spencer went into the radio room and after a moment Anthony Gaye emerged. Fraser and Eldridge were already donning oilskins and Gaye hurried to follow suit.

Before they left Armstrong drew Fraser quietly to one side.

"Bruce," he was less formal now that no one else was intended to overhear. "Approach that ship with caution. There's something peculiar about this business and I'm not happy."

"Neither am I, sir," Fraser admitted.

"Remember — constant radio contact.

That's why I'm sending Mister Gaye."

Fraser nodded and then left the bridge with Eldridge and Gaye. Armstrong went back to the window overlooking the slowly rolling expanse of the tanker's long deck and raised his night glasses again. He studied the distant *Rhineland* with a deep concentration which he did not intend to relax until he knew exactly what was wrong.

On the starboard boatdeck the lifeboat had been made ready for lowering. The tarpaulin covering had been removed and the blocks and chains knocked away so that the boat swung free. John Deverall was waiting with a dozen men to man the lifeboat and two teams to man the winches. He looked up as Fraser and his two companions approached across the catwalk from the main superstructure.

"Sorry, John," Fraser told him. "I'm to command the boat and the Captain wants you back on the bridge."

"Rather you than me." The Second Officer grinned honestly and indicated the long drop over the side. "You'll find it different down there." He turned up his collar against the gusting wind that still carried a few drops of rain. "What's the picture, anyway?"

"We still don't know. The Captain thinks she could be another *Marie Celeste*." Fraser smiled wryly.

"Then you'd best watch out for the long tentacles of the big sea monster — or was it little men from Mars?"

"I'll tell you when I get back."

Fraser climbed aboard and acknowledged the life jacketed and oilskin-clad men around him. His place was in the bows but he noticed that Big Henry Elliot, the ship's massive Geordie Bo'sun had taken up his position by the tiller in the stern. Ashore Big Henry was a married man with six children and a ten-pint capacity for draught guinness, but at sea he was stolid, sober and reliable. Fraser waited until Philip Eldridge had joined him and Gaye had made himself comfortable beside the lifeboat's radio, then he gave Deverell the order to lower away.

The deck of the *Monolith* was ninety feet above sea level and so the descent was long and slow. Armstrong had allowed the long bulk of the tanker to slew round slightly so that the seas were now breaking on the port bow and keeping the starboard side in the lee of the wind. Even so the seas were rough and when the keel of the lifeboat eventually struck the crest of a rising wave it did so with a violent shock. There was a second jerk as the wave fell and the boat was left swinging on the ropes for a few more seconds. Then the next wave was lifting them up again. Fraser shouted a command and released the block and snap hook of the forward rope. Simultaneously the Bo'sun released the stern rope and there was a brief moment of acute danger from the flailing blocks and lines. Then the lifeboat fell away and the third wave carried them back along the sheer wall of black steel.

There was another nerve-racking

minute of crashing and scraping while the crew did their best to fend the lifeboat away from the towering overhang of the hull, and then on his third attempt the Bo'sun started the auxiliary engine. Big Henry grabbed the tiller from one of the seamen and under his guiding hand the boat began to push forwards and turn away from its mountainous parent. Fraser waved a casual farewell to the deck far above and then turned to search for the *Rhineland*.

John Deverell's remark that they would find things different at sea level proved to be more than an understatement. The heavy seas that barely disturbed the *Monolith* caused the comparatively microscopic lifeboat to heave and plunge with alarming regularity. The boat rounded the great bows and once clear of the shelter of the hull they met the seas head on. The wind tore bursts of spray from the wave tops and hurled them in freezing squalls into their faces. The lifeboat butted its way forward, sliding from trough to trough as the long waves surged beneath the keel. Anthony Gaye crouched over his radio and succeeded in establishing contact with Alan Spencer in the radio room of the *Monolith*. The rest of the crew watched the *Rhineland* looming closer as the lifeboat battled its way slowly through the intervening seas.

Over the last quarter of a mile Fraser stood upright in the bows, taking a battering from the wind and spray, but watching intently as the still silent and motionless freighter took more distinct shape in the darkness. He used his night glasses as well as he was able, but holding any focus was difficult due to the violent pitching and rolling of the lifeboat. He finally gave up and relied upon his naked eyes, but on the *Rhineland* nothing moved.

"They must have abandoned her," Eldridge shouted as the rust-streaked hull of the freighter reared above them. "Otherwise they would be lining the rails by now."

"But there's still no sign of any damage," Fraser was puzzled.

There was bafflement on the faces of the seamen as they looked up at the empty and silent rails of the mystery ship. The Bo'sun cut back the engine to wait for orders and the lifeboat began to wallow more drunkenly than before.

"Mister Gaye," Fraser said grimly. "Radio the *Monolith* and tell them that there is no sign of life and still no indication of what has gone wrong." He looked to the stern of the boat. "Bo'sun, take us slowly round the stern to her starboard side."

"Aye, aye, sir," Big Henry leaned forward to raise the throttle on the engine and then moved the tiller hard over. The lifeboat swung round and began to circle the high stern of the *Rhineland*. Fraser noticed that the freighter's rudder blade and screw both appeared to be undamaged as they passed.

The lifeboat rounded the *Rhineland*

and encountered more heavy seas on her starboard side. Fraser searched for any signs of blackened superstructure, blistered paint or twisted metal but again there was nothing. The *Rhineland* was intact, rolling heavily on an even keel but perfectly seaworthy. Her starboard lifeboats were all hanging neatly from their davits.

"So they didn't abandon her," Eldridge said, and now his tone was perplexed.

Fraser frowned. There was something uncanny and threatening about this silent ship and he could sense the mounting tension in his crew. Gaye was making another negative report to the *Monolith* and that contact was strangely comforting now that they were hidden from the tanker's view.

Fraser looked for a way aboard and saw a rope ladder dangling from the freighter's well deck just aft of the bridge. It was an open invitation and he ordered the Bo'sun to manoeuvre the lifeboat towards it.

When they were alongside Fraser grabbed the ladder with both hands and gave it a good pull to ensure that it was secured aloft. The *Rhineland* was still a ghost ship, drifting silently in the darkness, but Fraser knew that he couldn't show any hesitation in front of his men. Also there was only one way to solve the mystery.

He ascended the rope ladder steadily and without haste and stepped on to the *Rhineland*'s empty deck. He stared around for a moment and then Philip Eldridge joined him. Together they moved towards the nearest companionway leading up to the bridge.

There was a sudden movement, both before and behind. Fraser stopped dead as the sharp, cold touch of steel jabbed at his throat and then he was staring down the long samurai blade into the grinning and bespectacled face of Koiso Takaaki.

★ ★ ★

"Welcome aboard, Chief Officer."

Fraser had to turn his head to find the owner of the voice, moving slowly with the point of the sword still pricking beneath his larynx. For the first time in his life he looked into the dark, hawk-nosed face of Hasan Bakarat, and he knew instinctively that this man was both ruthless and merciless. The Schmeisser machine pistol held almost casually in Bakarat's hands was a superfluous sign, for his nature was printed indelibly in his fierce black eyes.

Another samurai sword was touching the nape of Eldridge's neck, freezing the Third Officer on the spot, and Fraser saw more men with machine pistols moving up to line the deck rail and threaten the men in the lifeboat below.

Zakaria called out a sharp warning to Anthony Gaye that gave him no choice but to move away from the radio.

Bakarat was smiling. "Please, Chief Officer, do not make any fatal mistakes,"

137

he advised softly. "The Captain and Chief Officer of the *Rhineland* both offered resistance and they are both dead. That was unfortunate but not important, for we needed this ship for a short period only. The *Rhineland* was our bait for a bigger fish. Now it is the *Monolith* that is vital to our plan, and as she will prove a more difficult ship to handle I prefer — if it is possible — to keep all her deck officers alive."

Fraser stepped back half a pace, away from Takaaki's sword. Then he turned his shoulder to the Japanese and stared directly at Bakarat. Neither of them blinked.

"Where are the crew and the surviving officers of the *Rhineland*?" Fraser demanded.

"They are not important. You can forget them."

"They are important to me. They are the men I came to help."

"Chief Officer, do not let us have any foolish battle of will. My strength is eleven men, all armed with automatic

138

weapons. We command the *Rhineland* and now we control you and your lifeboat. Soon we will command the *Monolith*."

"You haven't a hope," Fraser said bluntly.

He felt a smarting pain against the side of his neck and when he looked round he was again looking down the long bright gleam of the samurai blade. The gleam was reflected in Takaaki's spectacles.

"You have no choice," the Japanese told him.

Bakarat lifted the muzzle of his machine pistol and prodded briefly at the front of Fraser's life jacket.

"You will radio the tanker," Bakarat ordered. "Tell them that there has been a serious explosion in the engine room of the *Rhineland*. Tell them that you are evacuating those who have been injured."

"And the injured men we take back to the *Monolith* will be your men with their automatic weapons carefully

139

concealed." Fraser spelled out the rest and shook his head. He finished slowly, "I won't do it."

"I have said that your death would be regrettable," Bakarat reminded him. "But I will kill you if you refuse."

Fraser felt the trickle of warm blood soaking into his collar. He felt the night wind on his face and the hostile presence of the waiting terrorists. He saw the fanatical faces of Bakarat and Takaaki and he could smell death and fear.

At the same time there were other pictures in his mind. He remembered the birthday twins Gillian and Julie scampering gleefully around the saloon of the *Monolith* only a few hours before. He thought of shy Mary Darling with her baby in her arms. He thought of all the five wives and six children aboard the tanker, and he knew that he could not take these monsters back to endanger all their lives.

"The deck of the *Monolith* is ninety feet above the level of the sea," Fraser said quietly. "There is no way that you can get your men on board without my help — and I refuse."

Bakarat stared into the square, rugged face, reading the iron determination in Fraser's hard grey eyes. He saw no possibility of compromise and realized that on this issue the Chief Officer was prepared to die rather than ferry his men aboard the tanker. Bakarat frowned as he weighed his options, and then he made his decision. He drove the steel butt of the machine pistol hard into Fraser's stomach. Fraser was taken completely by surprise and as he doubled forward Bakarat stepped back and cracked the gun barrel hard across the side of his head. Fraser crashed unconscious to the *Rhineland*'s deck.

Bakarat barely spared him a glance. Instead he turned to stare into the horrified eyes of Philip Eldridge.

"Your Chief Officer was a fool," he said. "I refrained from killing him only because I may need him at a later stage. Therefore you will command the lifeboat and take us all back to the tanker. You will send the radio message that I have already dictated to allay their suspicions, and you will add that the Chief Officer has had a minor accident. That will explain why you are in the position of command."

Eldridge was afraid. His mouth was dry and his heart was racing fast. He swallowed and then spoke one word. "No."

"You are only a junior officer," Bakarat told him contemptuously. "You I do not need. You I can afford to kill."

Eldridge looked down at Fraser spralled on the wet deck, hoping desperately for a sign of movement. He prayed that Fraser would struggle up to resume this nightmare responsibility, but his prayers went unanswered. Fraser lay still. Eldridge knew that he was sweating and that his fear showed, but Fraser had set him a precedent and he knew what he must say. He looked back into the waiting eyes of Hasan Bakarat.

"The answer is still no."

Bakarat felt anger, a blind impulse to lift his machine pistol and carry out his threat. That this stripling of a boy should continue to defy him was almost too much and his finger ached as he controlled it from tightening on the trigger. He had to retain his control because his talk was bluff, and for this moment he knew that he could not afford to kill the *Monolith*'s Third Officer.

Bakarat had to think. The capture of the *Rhineland* had been made easy by the fact that Zakaria and his group had previously established themselves on board amongst the crew. He had no such fifth column aboard the *Monolith* and so everything depended on getting his men on board before any suspicions could be raised on the tanker's bridge. Obviously the return of the lifeboat would be watched through binoculars and so the situation aboard the lifeboat had to appear normal with one of the two officers in the commanding position in the bows. Now that Fraser was unconscious Bakarat had put himself in the position where he did need Philip Eldridge.

The answer to the dilemma lay in the Third Officer's eyes. Bakarat saw courage there, but it was a desperate brand of courage. Eldridge was young and inexperienced, and unlike Fraser he could be broken to Bakarat's will. Bakarat smiled because he believed that he knew the way. He called out to Zakaria and instructed that one of the seamen from the lifeboat be brought up on to the freighter's deck.

The man who was chosen was a small, happy-go-lucky Geordie who was usually whistling when he worked on the *Monolith*'s deck. He was silent now as he stepped uncertainly aboard the *Rhineland* and there was terror in his eyes. Zakaria pushed him forward with his machine pistol and Bakarat ordered him coldly to kneel.

The little man looked helplessly at Fraser and then at Eldridge. Eldridge couldn't help him because he hadn't yet realized what was intended. Bakarat repeated his command and reluctantly the seaman got down on his knees.

"Look down at the deck," Bakarat told him.

The little man bowed his head, still uncomprehending.

Bakarat looked at Takaaki and the Japanese smiled. He extended a hand towards his friend Hayashi as though conferring a favour and it was Hayashi who took a double-handed grip on his long samurai sword. He raised the blade and struck with a powerful swing of his tensed wrists.

The blow was merciful in its accuracy and speed, but as Eldridge stared down at the decapitated man at his feet he felt violently sick.

"Now will you obey me?" Bakarat demanded. "Or do you prefer to watch another execution?"

★ ★ ★

On the bridge of the *Monolith* Hugh Armstrong sensed a movement at his elbow. He lowered his binoculars and for a second he closed his eyes which ached from the constant strain of gazing at the darkened blur of the *Rhineland* across half a mile of open ocean. Then he turned his head and looked at his Chief Radio Officer.

"A message from the lifeboat," Alan Spencer said tersely. "Apparently there has been a major explosion in the engine room of the *Rhineland*. Her Captain intends staying on board as long as possible, but because there's a danger of the ship drifting on to the Spanish coast he wants his injured transferred to the *Monolith*. The lifeboat is bringing them back," Spencer paused and then added. "The message was signed by Mister Eldridge, sir. He says that Mister Fraser slipped on a wet companionway and knocked himself unconscious. Mister Eldridge is bringing the boat back."

Armstrong stared at him. "Are you

sure that message was transmitted by Mister Gaye from the lifeboat."

Spencer nodded.

Armstrong's eyes were doubtful beneath his thick brows.

"I ordered constant radio contact. Did Mister Gaye explain why there has been a fifteen minute radio silence?"

"No, sir."

"Very well, Mister Spencer — keep listening."

Spencer nodded and hurried back to the radio room.

Armstrong lifted his night glasses and resumed his searching scrutiny of the German freighter. There were many things that were still unexplained and he was disturbed. There was no sign of life on the freighter's bridge and as yet he had seen nothing move on her decks. In the circumstances he did not need a lifetime at sea to tell him that something was wrong and he wondered what had really happened on the blind side of the ship where his vision was blocked by the superstructure.

He tensed as he saw the lifeboat reappear from behind the stern of the *Rhineland* and observed it closely. He counted eleven additional figures in the boat who were wrapped or draped in blankets, but although they appeared to be carefully huddled and protected he had the strange feeling that none of them were seriously hurt. Not one of them was badly slumped or doubled as though in pain. They were all too upright. Armstrong moved his glasses slightly and attempted to concentrate on the face of Philip Eldridge who was standing upright in the bows. The lifeboat was lifting and falling too erratically over the wave crests for him to be sure, but he thought that his Third Officer's boyish face looked unduly strained.

Armstrong finally lowered his glasses and turned to the Second Officer who stood beside him.

"Mister Deverell," he said quietly, "I believe that something is amiss. I do not think that Mister Gaye would deliberately neglect my direct order to maintain a continuous radio contact — and I am positive that an officer of Mister Fraser's experience would not simply slip and fall on a wet companionway."

He produced a key and held it out. His tone and his eyes were bleak.

"I propose to advocate caution, Mister Deverell. Please go into the chart room and unlock the rifles."

# 8

IN the forward cargo hold of the *Rhineland* Eric Weber hung awkwardly on to the steel-runged ladder beneath the hatchway, and with a large sheath knife borrowed from one of the seamen he attacked the thick boards of the hatch cover immediately above his head. Besides him, also hanging from the ladder with one foot and one hand and stabbing vigorously with another knife was the ship's Bo'sun. Below them Kesseler and the rest of the *Rhineland*'s crew watched anxiously.

More than an hour had passed since Bakarat had ordered the engines stopped and then confined them all in the hold. Under the threat of the machine pistols there was nothing that they could do except descend and then listen in darkness to the hatch cover being battered firmly down. Silence had finally told them that they were being left to their own devices and it was then that Weber had suggested that the sailors turn out their pockets for matches, cigarette lighters and knives.

They had cut strips of sacking from the cargo bales at their feet and in the flickering glow of the flames cast by burning these in careful succession they had sufficient light to start work in the main task of breaking out. Now the upper section of the hold was slowly filling up with smoke and men were beginning to cough and curse. Weber's eyes were smarting and his throat felt raw. Also his wrist ached but he continued to stab away with the knife. The hatch boards were solid timber six inches wide and an inch and a half thick, but already they had succeeded in breaking down a two foot length of one board. Now they were on the second board, splintering away long slivers from the edges and working their way into the centre. With every stab and twist Weber felt his knuckles banging against the Bo'sun, but so far they had avoided gashing each other with the sharp knives.

After five more minutes Weber had dug a hole wide enough to insert his knife and turn the blade full circle. He paused and then withdrew.

"Enough, Carl," he said hoarsely. "We can get the rope through now."

The Bo'sun hesitated and then nodded. He had been working as though he intended to reduce the whole hatch cover to splintered kindling and he returned his knife reluctantly to the sheath at his hip.

Kesseler passed them the rope which had been taken from one of the cargo bales. Weber threaded it through the rough hole he had cut, passed it over the weakened board and then down through the gap where the first board had already been removed. He made it secure with two tight half hitches and then looked down and nodded. Kesseler and a dozen burly sailors threw their combined weight on the rope.

On the second heave there was a violent crack as the damaged board snapped. It pulled partially away before the rope slipped off the jagged end and Kesseler and his tug-of-war team collapsed in a heap. However, they were all grinning with triumph. The rope was quickly handed up again to Weber who retied it further along the broken board. Kesseler and his men took up a new position, pulling from an angle instead of from directly below. The broken board bent downwards and backwards with their weight, and then with another pistol-shot crack it snapped again. The broken section hurtled down and Kesseler and his sailors ducked hurriedly to escape injury.

Weber cautioned them all to silence and waited a moment before he made his next move. There was no sound from the deck above and no indication that their activity had been heard. Their last barrier to freedom was the canvas covering stretched tight over the hatchway and at last Weber reached up with his knife and deftly slit it open.

Weber raised his head warily through the slit and looked around. The foredeck was deserted. He looked up to the bridge but nothing moved. He waited for a moment, listening uncertainly but hearing nothing except the wind, the growl of the sea and the eternal creaking as the *Rhineland* pitched and rolled. Finally he climbed out on to the hatch cover and helped the Bo'sun and Kesseler to join him.

The Second Officer crouched only for a moment before his instinct told him that the ship had been abandoned.

"Carl, get the others out," he ordered briefly.

The Bo'sun wiped sweat from his face and nodded. Kesseler and Weber left him and ran to the rail and immediately they saw the gigantic bulk of the supertanker lying less than half a mile off their port beam. They stared blankly for a moment and then Kesseler spotted the lifeboat that was now half way between the two ships.

"They are leaving us behind," he said angrily.

He raised both hands to his mouth and would have shouted after the boat if Weber had not clamped a warning hand on his shoulder.

"They won't come back, " Weber said grimly. "Obviously our Arab friends are now in command of that lifeboat. They have no further use for the *Rhineland*, but for some reason they do want that tanker." Weber's mind was racing, aware that he had to make recompense for his past mistakes, and desperately trying to consider every possibility.

"We are too late to warn the lifeboat," Weber continued. "If we attract their attention we will only let the Arabs know that we are free. Somehow we must warn the tanker so that they will be prepared." The answer came to him and he decided urgently: "We must get to the radio room."

"Wait, Eric!"

Weber had started to turn but Kesseler had realized suddenly that they had to deal with more than one emergency.

"Great God in Heaven, the ship is sinking! Can't you feel it? They must have opened the sea cocks before they left. They mean to scuttle the *Rhineland* exactly as they scuttled the fishing boat!"

Weber stared into his shocked face, but then Kesseler regained his composure and released Weber's shoulder.

"You see to the radio — I will attend to the ship."

Weber nodded and ran. Behind him he heard Kesseler issuing urgent orders to the emerging members of the *Rhineland*'s crew.

Weber raced up the campanionways to the bridge. The lights were still burning but the helm stood unattended, the polished spokes of the wheel turned by the idle whim of the sea. Weber ran past it and into the radio room and there he stopped. The room looked as though someone had gone mad with a sledgehammer or a fire-axe and every item of equipment was smashed.

Weber stared. He wanted to curse but that wouldn't help. He had to think. There had to be another way of warning the tanker. He returned slowly to the bridge and looked round, praying for inspiration. Then he saw the emergency flashlights that were stowed neatly in a rack and he smiled with relief. His memory for the morse code was shaky, but he was confident that he could remember enough to flash a message. He grabbed the nearest flashlight and ran out on to the open port wing of the bridge. Now he had no choice but to take the risk of being observed from the lifeboat and he began to signal.

Three seconds later the *Rhineland* was split asunder by an almighty explosion and Weber was hurled into the sea.

★ ★ ★

The sound of the explosion turned every head in the lifeboat. Philip Eldridge stared back over the dark waves and watched in horror as the *Rhineland* cracked vertically amidships to allow a great spearhead of flame to hurl itself skyward. It was as though a toy boat had been chopped in two by one blow of a monstrous axe and the bows and stern reared clear of the sea as her broken belly sagged into a boiling whirlpool of fire and steam. For a moment both halves of the doomed vessel seemed to writhe in agony and then as the great weight of the sea rushed in through the shattered bulkheads she began to sink rapidly. The flaming spear glowed vivid orange at the core and the red and yellow flames leaped through the steam and smoke. On the tilted foredeck microscopic men were hurled helplessly down into the holocaust.

"Bo'sun, turn her about!"

Eldridge found his voice and Big Henry Elliot leaned hard on the tiller. The lifeboat was almost swamped by the black wall of a wave as she turned broadside to the seas.

"No. Third Officer!"

Hasan Bakarat was seated close to Eldridge with a blanket thrown around his shoulders. The blanket also covered his arms and the Schmeisser machine pistol that was now thrust hard into Eldridge's groin.

"Before we left we opened the sea cocks and planted an incendiary device against the fuel tank in the engine room. We have no further need for that ship — and so there is no need for you to return."

"There could be survivors," Eldridge said in anguish. "I'm sure I saw men running on her decks."

"It does not matter," Bakarat said coldly. "They were meant to die. The lifeboat will proceed to the tanker."

In the stern of the boat Farraj was watching the Bo'sun. He lifted his

159

machine pistol slightly so that the black muzzle showed briefly through the shrouding folds of his blanket.

"You heard," Farraj warned. "You will turn back on to our former course!"

Big Henry glowered at him defiantly and waited to hear Eldridge.

Eldridge was again staring back over their heads at the *Rhineland*. He saw the stern half of the ship lurch sideways and then slide beneath the black Atlantic with a long, roaring hiss of steam. The bridge superstructure on the forward part of the ship still burned furiously, the flames lighting up the surrounding ocean for a radius of several hundred yards. Then the bridge began to settle lower in the water, there was another explosion but the flames were being extinguished as the second half of the ship expired with another long, slithering sigh beneath the waves.

The death throes of the *Rhineland* had been mercifully brief.

As the glow of the flames died Eldridge looked down at Bakarat.

"We must go back," he insisted. "It's the law of the sea! It's the law of humanity!" He searched desperately for an argument that could mean something to this blind fanatic and finished. "Captain Armstrong must be watching all this from the *Monolith*. There could still be survivors and he will *expect* me to go back and search the area. If we don't go back then he will know that I am not in command."

Bakarat frowned. This was a line of reasoning that he had forgotten and after a moment he nodded slowly.

"Perhaps you are right. I cannot afford to alert your Captain's suspicions until we are actually on board the tanker. So we will go back and search the area before he gives you a direct order to do so over the radio. We will search for fifteen minutes, but — " he smiled grimly " — do not bother to search too hard. Even if we find any survivors I do not intend to bring

161

them aboard this lifeboat. Our search will be just a small charade to deceive your Captain."

★ ★ ★

Eric Weber was sucked down into the black infinity of the Atlantic Ocean. The freezing shock of plunging beneath the waves had brought him back to consciousness but it had not yet enabled him to collect his scattered senses. His helpless downward momentum seemed determined to carry him right to the seabed and he was choking on the salt water that had forced its way violently into his mouth and nostrils. There was a thundering in his head and a merciless pressure round his chest and he knew that he was drowning. Feebly he struggled to move his arms and legs and his descent dragged to a halt. With brain, heart and lungs near to bursting he strove to claw his way back to the surface.

When at last his blonde head broke

above the waves he could only gasp and splutter for the first few minutes as he fought for air. The blackness was still in his brain and his basic instinct was merely to keep treading water as he was tossed up and down by the long rolling seas. When he did manage to open his eyes and look for the *Rhineland* he had already been carried up to two hundred yards away from her hull. The broken-backed freighter was sinking fast and he remained incapable of movement until she had vanished beneath the swirling waves. Fortunately the long swell of the sea continued to sweep him further and further away, so that when the *Rhineland* did take her final death dive he was well clear of the vast whirlpool of suction that she left behind.

There were no other bobbing heads around him and Weber knew with bitter certainty that Kesseler and all the others must have died. For a moment he wanted to weep for all the senseless slaughter, but the need to look for his own survival came first. He turned away and began to swim, and because there was no better alternative he swam in the general direction of the *Monolith*.

After a few minutes of lonely swimming he heard the engine of the approaching lifeboat. Hope flared in his heart and he waited for another wave crest to lift him high before he could see what he hardly dared to believe. The lifeboat was returning. Weber spat out a mouthful of salt water and filled his lungs with air ready to cry for help, and then his mind issued a sharp warning and he bit off the panic urge between his teeth. He remembered that Bakarat had arranged the destruction of the ship and that Bakarat had obviously intended that every soul on board must perish. Now Bakarat was controlling the lifeboat and it was certain that he had not suffered any change of heart or mind. If Bakarat was allowing the lifeboat to return then it would not be for the purpose of rescuing survivors, but more likely to ensure that there were no survivors who might be picked up by another vessel. Bakarat would want no witnesses to raise an early alarm.

Silently, with an effort of iron will, Weber watched the lifeboat go past. Then he again began to swim.

He soon realized that his own efforts were having little effect, but that the sea itself was carrying him directly towards the *Monolith*. Like some elongated everest of steel the supertanker loomed above him out of the black night, with her deck and superstructure lights seeming as remote as the invisible stars. As the motion of the waves washed him closer Weber's spirits sank lower. He began to appreciate that he had as much hope of being seen from the tanker's lofty deck as an ant trying to attract the attention of an astronaut. He stopped swimming in momentary despair, but it was impossible to do anything except move with the waves.

After fifteen minutes he was immediately below the stupendous bows which rose like an inverted black pyramid. A moment of agonized indecision gripped him as he saw that he had a choice of being smashed against the rivet-studded wall of steel or of being swept past the bows and on into the endless blackness of the ocean. The surge of a wave lifted him up and he was helpless in its watery grasp. The decision was not his to make and it seemed that the sea had decreed that he was to be flung in sacrifice on to the blunt knife of the bows. Then in the last seconds he was spared. The wave parted on either side of the bows and Weber was carried into the sheltered sea on the lee side of the tanker.

He swam along the thousand feet length of the enormous hull, shouting for help and knowing that he could not be heard. Despair filled him again, and then he heard the lifeboat coming back.

Weber held himself close to the hull and watched as the lifeboat rounded

166

the bows. He could distinguish the life-jacketed members of the boat's crew from the blanket-
huddled figures who could only be Bakarat and his terrorists, and he guessed that the Schmeisser machine pistols were also hidden under the blankets. Again he was convinced that if he revealed himself Bakarat would kill him, but at the same time the lifeboat was the only possible way of reaching the deck of the tanker ninety feet above.

He wrestled with his dilemma as he watched the lifeboat manoeuvring beneath the wire ropes and tackle blocks that still dangled down the tanker's side. He saw no choice but to throw himself on Bakarat's mercy and his time was running out. He saw Eldridge and Elliot catch the swinging tackle blocks and make fast and then Elliot cut the idling engine of the lifeboat. In that moment Weber saw a possibility of salvation.

Weber dived and swam hard towards

the lifeboat beneath the surface of the sea. When he came up he was only a yard from the boat's now motionless propeller. He grabbed for it and missed as the boat was lifted up, but then another wave gave him the impetus he needed. He clamped both hands on the propeller shaft just behind the blade, and as the lifeboat was winched up the *Monolith*'s side so Weber was also pulled up from the clutches of the hungry sea.

# 9

IN the bows of the lifeboat Bakarat was carefully watching Philip Eldridge, ensuring that the only hand signals the Third Officer made were directly related to the task of raising the boat. Farraj watched the Bo'sun, while Yotaro monitored the radio and kept check on Anthony Gaye. The remaining occupants were all gazing upward as the lifeboat ascended, and no one guessed that they now had an extra passenger dangling at arm's length from the propeller shaft beneath the boat.

The sea water streamed out of Weber's clothes and the biting wind cut through him like blades of ice. He was weak and weary after the effort of swimming in the rough seas and almost immediately he began to feel the pulling strain on his arms. He realized for the first time that the powerful explosion that had thrown him from the bridge of the *Rhineland* had left him with a number of hurts and minor burns. Now his left shoulder was a mass of searing pain where his full weight stretched the already bruised and wrenched muscles and he began to fear that he could never hang on long enough to reach the tanker's deck.

He watched the seemingly endless black cliff face of the hull moving past. The ascent of the lifeboat was excruciatingly slow and he gritted his teeth as he tried to shift his weight more on to his sound right shoulder. The fingers of his right hand began to slip on the smooth polished surface of the propeller shaft and a gasp of agony escaped as he had to swing back on his left arm. The black surface of the sea receded until the waves were far below, a fearful drop, but still there was no sign of the deck rails above. Weber's head hung back until his neck ached almost as much as his arms, but his desperately searching eyes saw nothing but the continuing infinity of the great steel plates.

Weber moved his head forward to look down at the wave tops that were now seventy feet below. If he dropped then he knew that in his present state he would be incapable of twisting his body into a controlled dive. The fall would probably kill him. There was no hope in looking down and so he tilted his head back again. The lifeboat was winched up foot by foot and at last he saw the white-painted deck rails of the tanker appear beneath the curved underside of the lifeboat's dripping hull.

Weber drew up his knees, kicked his legs forward and began to swing. The pain in his shoulder was all but unbearable and his hands began slipping around the propeller shaft, but with frantic determination he heaved his body backwards and forwards. On the fourth swing the lifeboat had lifted him level with the tanker's main deck and the momentum he had gained had to be enough. As his body flailed forward he released his grip on the propeller shaft and launched himself at the rails. He crashed heavily against the ship's side, his knees taking the first impact against the outside edge of the scuppers. He started to slip down the hull but then his chest slammed against the lower rail. The last drop of wind was driven from his lungs but by blind instinct he got one arm over the rail and hung on.

After half a minute he was able to haul himself over the rail and collapse in the scuppers on the *Monolith*'s deck. In both mental and physical terms he was totally exhausted and he made no further resistance as unconsciousness washed over him in one vast, long-delayed wave of submission to pain and darkness.

Above him the lifeboat had been winched up to her davits and was swinging into the boatdeck.

★ ★ ★

John Deverell had watched the lifeboat coming up and as yet he had seen nothing to alarm him. In fact the sudden explosion and the rapid sinking of the *Rhineland* had convinced him that the German vessel had been the victim of a natural disaster and so his suspicions were allayed. He commanded the boatdeck with a rifle in his hands but he was in no way prepared to use it. He regarded the rifle as an unnecessary burden that should have been kept locked in its wall case in the chart room.

The lifeboat came level with the boatdeck and Deverell ordered his sailors to go easy. In the same moment he thought he heard something heavy thump on to the main deck below but he was too busy to take any real notice. The lifeboat rose another two feet and he ordered the winches locked and the boat swung inward. He was anxious to help the wounded survivors from the lost freighter and took a step forward.

173

Philip Eldridge saw the rifle in the Second Officer's hands. In the same instant he felt the muzzle of Bakarat's machine pistol move sharply away from his groin.

"John," Eldridge cried desperately. "Drop the rifle."

Deverell stared at him, startled and uncomprehending. He had almost forgotten about the weapon he was holding.

"For God's sake, drop it," Eldridge repeated. "You haven't got a chance."

For an eternal second the scene was frozen. Deverell's sailors had their hands on the gunwhales of the lifeboat as they steadied her back into her resting place and they too stared with blank faces. No one in the lifeboat had moved, but Bakarat allowed his blanket to slip from his arms and shoulders. The black muzzle of the Schmeisser machine pistol was aimed at Deverell's belly.

Deverell realized that every one of the eleven blanket-shrouded figures was similarly armed. He had no wish to commit suicide and it was too late for anything else. Slowly the Second Officer realized that the captain's caution was justified, and with a mixture of guilt and gall he opened his hands. The rifle dropped down on to the deck boards at his feet.

Bakarat smiled and with shouts of triumph he and his men scrambled out of the lifeboat to begin the final stage of their attack upon the *Monolith*.

★ ★ ★

Armstrong was watching from the bridge with the second rifle slung across his shoulders. He saw Deverell knocked aside as the terrorists dashed across the narrow catwalk that connected the boatdeck to the main island of the superstructure and then he spun on his heel and ran back to the radio room. He stopped in the doorway and snapped briskly:

"Mister Spencer — the *Monolith* is under attack by a force of armed men! Transmit that message immediately on all possible wavelengths."

Spencer had his headphones clamped in position and sat immovable before his transmitters. His face was pale and he did not appear to have heard.

"Mister Spencer!"

Armstrong raised his voice sharply to begin again, but then Spencer removed his headset and looked up slowly. Armstrong stopped then, realizing that there was more bad news.

"I've just had a warning from the lifeboat, sir," Spencer said helplessly. "Somebody down there is monitoring every transmission I make. If I start to send out a distress call then they assure me that Mister Eldridge will be shot. If I continue the call then Mister Gaye will be shot. They state that there will be no mercy for any of the hostages they already hold."

Armstrong's face turned to stone. For thirty seconds he was silent and then his mouth cracked. Bitterly his words escaped.

"Cancel the message."

Spencer nodded and Armstrong turned and strode back on to his bridge.

★ ★ ★

The excitement of the great supertanker sliding to a halt, followed by the dramatic and clearly visible eruption of the *Rhineland*, had ensured that everyone on board the *Monolith* was wide awake, including the women and children. Jane Campbell had found it impossible to get her two sons back to sleep, especially four-year old Angus who was precocious, slightly spoiled and determined to see everything that was happening. Her husband had been called away to the engine room and so Jane finally wrapped up both boys and took them into the wide alleyway that ran the full width of C deck. From the windows on the starboard side they could look down on the boatdeck and watch for the return of the lifeboat. Jane was in her dressing gown, but when Sue Deverell and Elizabeth Fergusson joined her they were both fully dressed.

"Why has Uncle John got a gun?" was one of the innumerable questions that Angus asked while they waited, but it was one that none of the women could answer. They were puzzled but not unduly perturbed.

They watched as the lifeboat was at last swung back on board and noted the additional figures from the *Rhineland* huddled beneath their blankets.

"Some of those poor devils must be hurt," Elizabeth said. "The Captain's no doubt been too busy to order it so we'd best clear the saloon and make ready to receive them."

Sue nodded agreement. "We'll want all the medical equipment laid out, and clean towels and sheets for bandages."

They turned away to prepare, but they had only taken a few steps along the alleyway when Angus uttered a shrill squeal of excitement and Jane a sharp cry of alarm. Sue ran back to look down through the window and was just in time to see her husband swept aside as Bakarat and his men stormed across the catwalk below.

For a few seconds the three women were too amazed to react and then it was too late. Once across the catwalk Bakarat led the way up the ascending companionways in a fast rush. He saw the frightened faces and the window and without hesitation kicked open the door into the interior of the ship. The group leaders Zakaria and Takaaki crowded in behind him with five more of their men. Jane Campbell clutched her two boys close and screamed.

Bakarat saw that the blonde woman was hysterical and useless to him. So he rammed the muzzle of his machine pistol into Sue's stomach.

"There are five women and six children," he said harshly. "We know that! Where are the others?"

Sue stared into his face. Terror welled up inside her but she couldn't tell him. She lied weakly.

"I don't know."

"Of course you know — you will lead us to their cabins." Bakarat reached out one hand and tore the shrieking Ian from his mother's grasp. "You will tell me quickly or I will kill this child!"

Sue was incapable of speech. She desperately wanted to faint but couldn't.

Takaaki transferred his machine pistol to his left hand and with his right he drew his sword from behind his shoulder. He held the blade poised over the tousled red head of the three-year old boy.

"I will lead you," Elizabeth Fergusson said quickly. She put her bare hand against the flat of the blade and pushed it away. The Japanese looked into her grey face and smiled.

Bakarat also smiled and nodded to Zakaria. Their movements had all been planned and it was Zakaria's group that had the responsibility of rounding up the prize hostages. Zakaria grabbed Elizabeth's shoulder and Jabril took a firm grip on Sue. Then without any waste of time the group moved off to complete their haul.

Bakarat retained his grip on Ian, tucking the writhing child underneath his left arm as he continued his dash to the bridge. Seeing her younger son carried away Jane needed no real inducement to follow and was hustled along at Bakarat's heels with Angus still clutched to her breast. Takaaki, Hayashi and Shefik followed close behind with their machine pistols at the ready, for it had been decided in advance that a joint team of Arabs and Japanese would share the glory of capturing the tanker's bridge.

Armstrong was waiting grimly at the head of the highest companionway. The rifle in his hands pointed down but when he saw the sobbing woman and the two struggling boys he made no attempt to fire.

Bakarat grinned up into his face, and

then he handed Ian over to Takaaki. Still smiling insolently, and with both hands holding the Schmeisser machine pistol, he climbed slowly up the last companionway. Armstrong waited for him and in that moment either could have killed the other. Bakarat saw the controlled fury blazing in the hard eyes beneath the gold-peaked cap, but he calculated that he was safe while he held the women and children. He held out his left hand.

"Give me the rifle, Captain. Alone it is worth nothing against eleven submachine guns. Your ship is mine, and the fate of the *Rhineland* should be enough to tell you that nothing can stand in my way."

Armstrong stood rigid for a moment, and then slowly he shifted his gaze to look down over Bakarat's shoulder. All that registered was the blonde woman in the dressing gown with her plump face streaked with tears.

"Release Mrs Campbell," he ordered coldly.

Shefik hesitated. Bakarat offered him no guidance but slowly he took his hand away from Jane's shoulder. Immediately she snatched Ian back from Takaaki and then crouched to hold both her children close.

Armstrong's face did not relax, but he lowered the rifle. He ignored Bakarat's waiting hand and threw the rifle down to Shefik. He didn't stop to watch the thin-faced Arab stagger back against the rail with the unexpected blow. Instead he turned stiffly and walked back on to his bridge.

Bakarat followed him, with Takaaki and Hayashi ascending the companionway fast on his heels.

On the bridge Alan Spencer and the three seamen on duty waited uncomfortably. Armstrong looked to the Radio Officer.

"Mister Spencer, please escort Mrs Campbell and her sons back to their cabin."

"To the saloon — " Bakarat corrected him. "From this moment all the wives and children on board this ship will be held in the saloon."

Armstrong turned to face him and Bakarat continued:

"You must appreciate, Captain, that this ship is now under the command of combined forces for the liberation of Palestine. I am Hasan Bakarat. I represent a Palestine commando group. My good friend Koiso Takaaki leads a group from the Red Star Army of Japan. I am in overall command." He paused for effect. "You must also appreciate, Captain, the fact that all the women and children on board this ship have become our hostages to ensure the continuing good behaviour of yourself, your officers and your crew. They will be kept under constant guard, but as long as we meet with no difficulties they will not be harmed."

"What exactly do you want?" Armstrong demanded grimly.

"First a radio message must be sent," Bakarat told him carefully. "It is possible that other vessels or

184

shore stations may have picked up the *Rhineland*'s distress call, and obviously you will have passed on the information that the *Monolith* is giving assistance. We do not want the world to wonder what has happened next and so you will tell them. The *Monolith* will transmit a message to say that the *Rhineland* has unfortunately been lost after a major explosion in her engine room, and that all possible survivors have been brought aboard the tanker. The truth is after all the best concealment for those additional factors that we do not wish to be known."

"And if I refuse?" Armstrong said bluntly.

"You are in no position to refuse — remember your women and children!"

Armstrong folded his arms across his chest. His hands were balled into massive fists and it was the only way to keep them still.

"Alright, the message will be sent — then what do you want?"

Bakarat shrugged. "Nothing that is

very difficult. You will resume your original course and the *Monolith* will continue her voyage to Rotterdam. Your officers and crew will attend to their normal duties. Radio messages will be sent and received as usual, although of course there will be a permanent guard in the radio room to monitor all calls. Apart from the presence of myself and my companions everything will be routine."

He smiled as he finished: "When we reach Rotterdam in thirty-six hours time, no one outside this ship will be able to suspect that anything is wrong."

# 10

IN London it was a cold grey morning, one of those perverse April days that determined to relapse into winter. Rain threatened and in the Counter-Terror office overlooking the grumbling traffic in Victoria Street Mark Nicolson and Alexander Gwynne-Vaughan reflected the mood of the weather. They were studying the latest batch of reports from their contemporaries throughout Europe and there were visible trends that gave them cause for concern.

"Gaiani seems to have run into a dead end," the Co-ordinator said with regret. "He did a good job in tracking down Bakarat's girl friend but then she killed herself in a futile attempt to escape. She was Bakarat's only indiscretion and the others seem to have made no outside contact at all. I'm afraid that our sources of information in Rome have run dry."

"And Madrid?" Nicolson posed the question without enthusiasm.

"A minimum of progress. I had another long telephone conversation with Ramondez last night. He feels sure that he's found the place where Bakarat and his two friends stayed when they first arrived in Madrid. It's a small hotel called the Hotel Carmen in the old part of the city. Three Arabs stayed there for five days and then two days ago they paid their bill and left. Ramondez has checked out the airport and he's confident that they didn't fly out. He's also found the time to make some limited enquiries at Madrid's central railway station. A ticket clerk there does remember serving three men of Arab nationality on the day that Bakarat and his friends booked out of the Hotel Carmen. They approached him separately but they all booked one way tickets to Zaragoza."

"Zaragoza," Nicolson repeated thought-fully. "That means they were moving north — could they be heading back into France?"

"Perhaps — " Gwynne-Vaughan considered the suggestion. "But I doubt if they have yet made any attempt to cross the frontier. Remember that Major Cassin was alerted to that possibility the moment we knew that these men had gone to earth in Spain. We had our early difficulties in France, but now the Paris office under Cassin is one of the most efficient in the whole of the Counter-Terror network. If Bakarat and his group try to cross the Pyrenees then Cassin will know — and we will be informed."

"It would not surprise me to receive that information at any moment," Nicolson said. He indicated the reports that lay on his desk and continued: "Everything we've received over the past few days seems to indicate a general drift of terrorist movement toward Holland."

189

Gwynne-Vaughan frowned and smoothed a forefinger carefully over his moustache, a sign that his mind was preoccupied. "That's what is really worrying me, Mark. Yesterday it was a report from Brussels — two Arabs stopped on the Belgian frontier with Holland and arrested with revolvers in their possession. And the day before Cassin's men in Paris picked up another two-man team that had flown in from the Lebanon. They were clean when they were checked in at Orly Airport, but a double-check twelve hours later when they attempted to leave Paris in a hired car showed that somewhere they too had collected revolvers and ammunition — and they were driving north when they were stopped."

"And there's another report this morning from Inspector Brenner in Munich," Nicolson added grimly. "Some of the doubtful characters he's had under observation are also on the move."

Gwynne-Vaughan took the report

and read it through, frowning as he did so. Then he stood up and walked slowly over to the window where he stared down absently at the Victoria Street traffic. He was a big, heavy man lost in thought and his finger was again smoothing his moustache. Most of his early military and diplomatic career had been served in the Middle East, including five years as Security Chief for one of the larger British embassies, and so he knew the problems, pressures and mentality of the Arab world as well as any non-Arab could possibly know them. It was for this reason that he had been appointed to the highest post in the new Counter-Terror organization. Now he drew upon the deep well of all his past knowledge and experience as he tried to understand the meaning behind this latest wave of Arab movement in Europe.

Mark Nicolson remained at his desk, turning over the reports of the past week. His policeman's brain was searching for a common factor and only one stood out with unmistakable prominence. Holland was the centralizing focus for all the groups on the move and Amsterdam was the host city for the Mutual and Balanced Force Reductions Conference that was now beginning. There were twelve delegations of top-ranking diplomats from Canada, the U.S.A. and Western Europe, plus seven Communist delegations from behind the Iron Curtain, all congregated in the first class hotels of Amsterdam, and one or all of those Very Important People were possible targets.

The two men were still deep in silent thought when a Police Constable entered with another report.

"This has just come through, sir," he addressed Nicolson. "Red priority from Inspector Helders."

Gwynne-Vaughan intercepted the Constable and took the double page transcript before it could be placed on the desk. He did so without apparent haste but the very fact that he had stepped forward betrayed his hidden

192

concern. He read the report through and then passed it over to Nicolson.

"Another incident," he said grimly. "This time on the Dutch-German frontier."

Nicolson read the report in turn, slowly and trying to visualize the events that had occurred only an hour before.

A Citroen car containing two men of Arab nationality had approached a Dutch frontier post from Germany. The German police had let the Citroen pass after a cursory inspection, but exiting one country was always easier than entering another and the Dutch Police had been more thorough. The car had been detained for fifteen minutes and the two Arabs had been closely questioned. The boot of the car had been opened and searched and one alert customs officer had examined the spare wheel. The Citroen was brand new but scratches on the rim of the wheel showed that the tyre had at some stage been removed and replaced. The Dutch Police began to remove it again and at that stage the two Arabs had panicked. Both men had suddenly reached for loaded automatics that had been taped underneath the front seats of the car and a violent gun battle had erupted. One Dutch policeman had been shot dead before the two Arabs tried to run back to the German side of the frontier. The German guards had drawn their own weapons and caught in a cross fire both the Arabs had died. The suspect spare wheel had later been found to contain twelve hand grenades packed in cotton wool.

The account was precise but brief, and signed by Inspector Dirk Helders, Counter-Terror Section Head for Amsterdam.

Nicolson had increased his reading speed towards the end of the second page, but there was a phrase that had struck a familiar chord in his mind and he went back to it.

"No justice for Palestine — no peace for the world." He read the words aloud slowly and then looked up at Gwynne-Vaughan. "Those were the last words uttered by one of those Arabs before he died. Helders must have sensed that they were important or he wouldn't have included them in the report — but where have we heard them before?"

Gwynne-Vaughan stared at him and then enlightenment broke over them together.

"That last report from Paris," Gwynne-Vaughan said.

"Here it is!" Nicolson already had the report to hand. "The two men Paul Cassin picked up in Paris were questioned non-stop for twelve hours. They refused to talk until one of them spat a slogan into the face of one of Cassin's aides. The words were — 'No justice for Palestine — no peace for the world!'"

"Then there is a link," Gwynne-Vaughan decided. "All of this sudden surge of terrorist movement is co-ordinated to one specific end!"

"And it has to be the conference,"

Nicolson said with equal conviction. "The future peace of the Western world could well be determined by the success of these talks between N.A.T.O. and the Warsaw Pact. If the conference could be disrupted, or one of the leading delegations assassinated, then any lessening of military tension in Europe could be retarded by a dozen years." His face paled. "Can you imagine what might happen if the Russian delegates were hit? The Warsaw Pact nations might decide that we had deliberately allowed it to happen — or even have had a part in it — we could be one giant step nearer to World War Three."

"That's the security nightmare that accompanies every high level visit from a foreign state," Gwynne-Vaughan said grimly. "And in Amsterdam at the present moment it's multiplied by twenty-nine."

"Are you happy with Dutch security?"

"I have confidence in Dirk Helders, the security blanket he's arranged is as good as any. Plus most of the major delegations will have their own immediate security agents. I don't think that any more can be done, and remember that Counter-Terror is proving effective and that we've already picked up three possible assassination teams."

Gwynne-Vaughan paused there to consider the other side of the picture, and then he admitted:

"Despite all that I'm not exactly complacent. We know that in today's world with millions of people legitimately crossing frontiers every day it is impossible to maintain a perfect security screen. There may be other assassination teams that have succeeded in slipping into Holland, or who have been living there for months. We also have to consider the fact that all these movements are linked, which suggests some kind of master plan. What worries me is the nagging feeling that there is something more than just the movement of the assassination teams.

If they are all intended to strike together then there must be some kind of signal to start the operation — possibly some kind of major diversion that will give them more freedom to act."

Nicolson frowned. "You mean another form of terrorist attack — something spectacular that could throw a disastrous weight on the security forces?"

Gwynne-Vaughan nodded and again they were both thoughtful.

# 11

BRUCE FRASER recovered consciousness and opened his eyes. The bright light made him blink and there was a dull pain across the side of his head. The pain started in his temple and throbbed back in slow waves above his left ear. As the dark mist cleared from the corridors of his brain his memory returned. He made a sudden effort to struggle upright but a firm hand pushed him down.

"Elizabeth, he's awake."

Fraser recognized the voice and then the face of Sue Deverell. She was kneeling over him and it was her hand on his shoulder. Then Elizabeth Fergusson appeared at her side.

"They brought you back aboard the *Monolith*, Bruce," the older woman explained briefly. "You're in the saloon."

Fraser recognized the elaborate white

shell pattern of the ceiling. He shifted his head slightly and saw the carved wooden panelling that framed the bar with the bottles and glassware sparkling within. He realized that he was lying on the floor on a pile of blankets and pillows and that there was a thick layer of white bandage around his head. Then Elizabeth was speaking again.

"Bruce, move your right hand."

Fraser obeyed, lifting his hand clear of the blankets.

"Good! Now flex the fingers."

Again Fraser complied.

Elizabeth Fergusson smiled. "The left side of your brain controls the right side of your body," she explained, "but there's no sign of brain damage. You've got a nasty cut and some bruising across the left side of your head, but I think you'll be alright if you rest."

Fraser had no intention of resting and made a determined effort to sit up. This time he succeeded and moved Sue's restraining hand aside. Looking past her he saw the frightened blue eyes of Mary Darling. Mary was holding her baby in her arms, and behind her Fraser saw Jane Campbell and Jackie Spencer, both with their own children grouped close around them. Also positioned around the saloon were four of the dark-faced Arab terrorists whom he had last seen on board the *Rhineland*. Two of them sat relaxed but with their Schmeisser machine pistols close at hand on the tables before them, while their companions had their weapons cocked and levelled.

"What's happening?" Fraser demanded.

"We're all being held hostage," Sue told him quietly. "They haven't got enough men to police the whole ship — but they believe that while they can control the bridge and threaten us they will be safe."

Zakaria moved forward to boast: "We have taken your ship, Chief Officer. Here, I am in command. If you wish to ask questions you may address them to me."

Fraser stared at him for ten cold seconds and then looked back to the women.

"Are any of you hurt?"

They shook their heads with varying degrees of uncertainty.

"We're just having to put up with the inconvenience of being confined to the saloon," Sue continued. "If one of us has to leave then a guard escorts us to where we're going and then brings us back. The mothers are not allowed to accompany their own children, but apart from that there's no real hardship."

Fraser guessed that their situation was not quite as easy as she maintained, but for the moment there was nothing that he could do to help. He looked at the tiny, fretting faces of the children and knew that while they were at risk his hands were effectively tied. He struggled to his feet and Sue and Elizabeth helped him to stand.

"I have to report to the bridge," Fraser said grimly.

Zakaria tightened his thir.
was angry at the manner in
command had been ignored,
knew that Bakarat wanted th
Officer alive. For a moment he stood
in the doorway, blocking Fraser's exit.
Then, with his machine pistol still
levelled, he stepped aside.

"Jabril," he said curtly, "take the
Chief Officer to the bridge."

Fraser left the saloon with Jabril
walking warily two paces behind.
He moved aft along the alleyway
and stepped out on to the edge of
open deck that looked on to the
towering black girth of the funnel
that occupied most of the poop deck
of the island superstructure. Heavy grey
clouds dragged their sagging bellys and
twisted tails across the sky and all
around were sullen grey seas. It was
a bleak morning that showed no real
improvement in the weather and when
Fraser looked at his wristwatch the
hands stood at eight-thirty. That meant
that he had been unconscious for a little

than four hours.

The *Monolith* was under way, rolling steadily and maintaining her normal speed. Fraser gripped the rail for a moment to breathe in the fresh tang of the Atlantic air. The strong wind blew the last of the cobwebs away from his mind and when he turned and ascended the sucession of steel companionways to the bridge there was a returning briskness to his stride.

He found Armstrong in command. The Captain turned from his position by the helmsman and for a brief moment the strained creases relaxed around his mouth and eyes.

"Mister Fraser, are you fit?"

"Fit enough," Fraser acknowledged, "Mine is a hard head to crack."

"I am pleased to hear that, Chief Officer." Bakarat moved into view, smiling coldly with his machine pistol in his hands. "I fear that the Captain's stamina may not last for the entire voyage and so I may need you to take command while he sleeps. I am well aware that the number of ships using the English Channel can create considerable hazards for a vessel of this size, and so one of her senior officers must be wide awake at all times. I have no wish to run this ship aground, or to have her involved in a collision."

Fraser took a step towards him and then stopped. He wanted to close his hands around Bakarat's throat but this was not the time. He looked left and right and saw the dark bullfrog face of Farraj and the glittering spectacles of Takaaki, plus the machine pistols that were aimed at his belly. Then he looked to Philip Eldridge who was standing watch by the radar screens.

"So you brought them aboard," he said bitterly.

The note of censure brought a dark flush to the Third Officer's cheeks, but before he could answer Armstrong intervened.

"Mister Eldridge had no choice," The Captain said quietly. "They decapitated one of our seamen with a sword."

Fraser stared at him, then at Bakarat. For a moment he refused to believe that even this monster could be so ruthless. Bakarat shrugged and made no denial. Fraser looked at Takaaki, noting the sword slung across the shoulders of the Japanese, and then he accepted that nothing was beyond these people. There was no butchery or evil at which they would cry halt.

He turned back to Eldridge and said quietly,

"I'm sorry, Philip."

Eldridge merely nodded and stared down at his radar screens.

★ ★ ★

The *Monolith* had now rounded Cape Finisterre to begin the long crossing of the Bay of Biscay. The gale warnings that had been forecast the night before had still not materialized and while the weather was reasonably calm Armstrong ordered his entire crew to assemble on the stern deck. There he addressed them briefly from the overlooking rail of deck with Bakarat and Takaaki standing threateningly on either flank. On B deck above Zakaria had paraded the hostages and the terrorists showed their full force and range of weapons.

Armstrong's speech was bitter and brief, and scorning the use of a loud-hailer he shouted it out against the wind. He explained what had happened and grimly underlined the fact that the women and children were now being held to ransom for the good behaviour of every man on board. To conclude he could only order them all to accept the situation and carry out their normal duties in regard to the maintenance and safety of the ship.

"The *Monolith* is proceeding to Rotterdam," he finished. "There I can only assume that these people have some kind of ultimatum to make to the authorities. Whatever they demand we can only hope that a satisfactory outcome can be negotiated. In the meantime my duty is to safeguard the ship and the lives on board."

There were a number of hard and uncompromising faces among the ranks of seamen and engineers, but there were no questions. They all knew what had happened to the *Rhineland*, and there was not a man on board who did not have some degree of affection for the children who had once romped carefree along the decks of the *Monolith*. Armstrong thanked them and turned away and Bakarat and Takaaki followed him back to the bridge. The two terrorist leaders had sensed that any added words of their own would only have antagonized the crew and in return for Armstrong's co-operation they had remained silent.

Zakaria and his group shepherded their charges back inside and the men on the lower deck slowly began to disperse. Fraser held back to watch them move below but then the Bo'sun caught his eye. Big Henry hesitated for a moment and then he slowly ascended the companionway to where

Fraser stood by the rail.

"What is it, Mister Elliot?"

"The Captain said to carry on regular maintenance, sir," Big Henry spoke carefully because they were both aware that Shefik had paused nearby to listen. "Does that mean that you want the hands to continue painting the deck rails on the starboard side?"

Fraser looked up at the grey skies. "The weather could turn nasty so you'd better leave it. Find them some work below."

"Very good, sir," The Bo'sun began to suggest alternative means of keeping the crew busy and Shefik lost interest. When the Arab had moved away Big Henry lowered his tone and said quickly.

"We've got a man down in the crew's mess, sir — the Third Officer from the *Rhineland*." He explained hurriedly how Eric Weber had succeeded in getting aboard the *Monolith* and finished: "When he found the strength to crawl he made his way down to us, sir. I thought you ought to know."

Fraser thought rapidly. The presence of one survivor from the *Rhineland* made no difference to their present situation, but it was a card for the future.

"Keep him well hidden, Bo'sun," Fraser advised. "For the moment these bloody-handed murderers have got us toeing the line — but if we can eventually bring them to trial then your friend Weber will be a major witness."

★ ★ ★

In the saloon Elizabeth Fergusson took charge, ordering breakfast served as usual and insisting that they all eat, including the guards. Zakaria was compliant but watchful. He allowed no man to enter the saloon except one steward, but the galley staff were free to take meals to the ship's officers in their cabins or on the bridge. Consequently breakfast was a strained and difficult meal. Elizabeth ate heartily, an example which Sue tried to follow. The others ate with less enthusiasm and they all endeavoured to coax the children. Mary had no appetite at all beyond a glass of grapefruit juice and one cup of coffee.

When the plates had been cleared away Elizabeth approached Zakaria. There were many long and empty hours ahead and she pointed out that they needed such things as jigsaw puzzles, drawing books and crayons to amuse the children. The tall Arab hesitated for a moment and then gave her permission to leave the saloon. She returned five minutes later with her arms full of books, puzzles and games.

They made a determined effort to keep the little ones entertained, but beneath the ugly eyes and gun muzzles of their guards it was not easy. The twin girls would normally be absorbed for hours over a picture book and a box of paints, but now they had no real interest and their frightened eyes shifted frequently as they sent sidelong glances around the room. Julie finally gave up and went over to her mother and began to cry softly. Gillian wanted her daddy. Sue and Jane tried to help the boys with their favourite jigsaw, but even with the red and green railway train which they had put together many times before the pieces refused to fit. The boys became increasingly more irritable, usually they could not get through a morning without a vigorous three-way wrestling match but now they were sulky and subdued. The women found that any attempts at conversation amongst themselves were broken into stiff fragments as the presence of the silent guards began to wear at their nerves.

Slowly and inexorably the tension began to mount.

The mid-day meal was a temporary relief and from the galley the cooks and stewards did their best to tempt the prisoners. Food aboard the *Monolith* was always of first class standards, but now the plates were arranged with extra care. The women were not hungry but they ate to encourage the children, and because Elizabeth again insisted that they must. Only Mary Darling refused, after picking listlessly at her plate with a fork in one hand. She had nursed the baby all through the morning and was reluctant to let him out of her arms.

During the afternoon they made renewed efforts with the puzzles and games. A drawing competition failed to excite and ludo and snakes and ladders both proved a dull flop. Sue read them the story of the *Three Billy Goats Gruff* but she was too self conscious and the children were not listening. Gradually the sharp, unblinking stares of the four Arabs were causing the women varying degrees of embarrassment. Sue Deverell knew that she was an attractive woman and for the first time in her life she wished that she was not.

The tension returned and the coiled spring wound ever tighter.

There had been no women on board the *Rhineland* and the four Arabs were plainly lustful. Sue could feel their eyes undressing her and wished that she had worn a longer skirt. Jackie Spencer was equally uncomfortable and now kept the twin girls close beside her.

Towards mid-afternoon Jabril left the saloon. When he returned he paused for a moment beside the table where Sue was trying to interest the boys in another jigsaw. Jabril's hand rested on her shoulder and Sue froze. The hand moved to stroke her bare arm and she quickly recoiled. Jabril frowned and his companions laughed. Then Jabril shrugged and moved away with an ironic smile.

Zakaria returned the smile and said nothing. The tall Arab could feel the same awakening urge, but he was not interested in Sue Deverell. Dark-haired girls were plentiful in his own land, and even girls with ripe breasts and white thighs like this one he had known before. What really fascinated him were the blue eyes and the long honey-blonde hair of Mary Darling. Zakaria liked his women to be young, and despite the baby this one was soft and trembling like a child.

Another hour passed. The baby was restless and finally Elizabeth Fergusson offered to nurse him for a while. Both she and Sue had made previous offers which Mary had refused but this time the offer was accepted. Mary was still reluctant but she didn't want to be rude, and so she allowed Elizabeth to take the baby from her arms.

Zakaria watched her. Without the baby it would be impossible to guess that she was old enough to be married. A man could imagine her to be a virgin, and that was how Zakaria wanted to imagine her. He wanted her badly and he asked himself the basic question — why not? He was in command here and his will was absolute. What difference could it make to the success of their operation if he chose to enjoy this woman?

Zakaria hesitated for a few more minutes but the desire and the opportunity were too ripe to be missed. He made up his mind and approached with a casual smile. The machine pistol was relaxed at arm's length in his right hand. His left hand he held out to Mary and said simply,

"Come!"

The blue eyes stared at him, filled with fear and protest.

"Come," Mary repeated weakly. "Come where?"

"With me, somewhere comfortable." Zakaria chuckled. "To a cabin perhaps — does it really matter where?"

Mary tried to pull back but he grabbed her arm and pulled her fiercely to her feet. Elizabeth and Sue shouted angrily and tried to intervene but the muzzles of the machine pistols thrust them back. Zakaria was grinning and gaining added delight from the pure terror of Mary's frantic struggles.

"You can't!" Elizabeth cried. She made another effort to get near him but Jabril pushed her down on to a chair.

"Who is to stop me?" Zakaria said carelessly. "I am in command here."

"No," Mary begged him. "Please, don't. Please, please — "

Zakaria ignored her and dragged her to the door. His fingers were like iron claws crushing her arm and even when she slipped to her knees and held back with all her weight she could not break free. She beat at him with one fist but Zakaria only laughed. The tears flowed down her white face and her pleas reached hysteria. The children ran screaming to their mothers.

"Leave her alone!" Sue implored. Then her fears for the children and for Mary's sanity overcame her revulsion and she added desperately. "If you must have a woman, take me! I won't struggle, I promise. Please let her go."

Zakaria paused to show his teeth in a wild, flashing grin.

"At this moment I do not want a willing woman," he told her scornfully. "I want a woman who fights and makes love interesting. If you are so

eager one of the others can have you
— afterwards, when I return!"

Again he hauled Mary Darling
towards the door and her screams
drowned out those of the children.

★ ★ ★

Philip Eldridge had left the bridge at
noon and had been allowed to return to
his own cabin to rest. He lay awake on
his bunk, unable to sleep. Guilt haunted
him for he had brought the terrorists to
the *Monolith* and he could not forget
that brief look of censure he had seen
in Fraser's eyes. Now he re-lived those
moments on the deck of the *Rhineland*,
searching for ways in which he might
have acted differently. His share of
responsibility for all that had already
happened weighed on his reason, and
then his mental anguish was abruptly
interrupted by the screaming from the
deck below.

Eldridge left his cabin at a run
and took the nearest descending

companionway in three downward leaps. Four more strides took him to the double doors of the saloon and he crashed them open. Zakaria wheeled to face him, still holding Mary in one hand and his machine pistol in the other. Eldridge knew instinctively what was happening and without any thought or hesitation he balled a fist and dealt the Arab a resounding crack on the jaw.

All the Third Officer's weight and all the pent-up misery and bitterness in his heart exploded in the punch and Zakaria was smashed sprawling to the deck. Mary fell on top of him and for a split second Eldridge stood alone in the doorway, his fists still clenched and fury written on his face.

Then Jabril squeezed the trigger of his Schmeisser machine pistol and the burst of bullets hit Eldridge in the stomach with all the speed and power of an express train.

Bruce Fraser heard the muffled sound of gunfire from the bridge. He handed over command to John Deverell and then with Bakarat and Takaaki running fast at his heels he hurried below. The three of them burst into the saloon together and it was only the presence of the two senior terrorist leaders that saved Fraser from being shot in turn.

Jabril still held the smoking machine pistol pointed at the doorway.

Eldridge was dead and Zakaria was getting to his feet and wiping the blood from the side of his mouth.

Bakarat cursed Zakaria with savage questions in Arabic.

Under the outburst Zakaria faltered and mumbled something that was obviously unsatisfactory.

Fraser helped Mary to her feet and then looked to the other women.

"What happened here?"

Elizabeth Fergusson told him as calmly as possible.

Fraser turned slowly on the tall Arab with the bleeding mouth. His own hands balled into fists as his right elbow drew back. Bakarat stepped up from behind him and his machine pistol dropped in a warning barrier across Fraser's chest.

Fraser held himself in check, knowing that it was pointless to end up dead beside Eldridge. He turned to meet Bakarat's eyes but Bakarat lashed out at his own man and for the second time Zakaria was knocked violently to the deck. Bakarat then levelled his machine pistol at a point between Zakaria's hate-filled eyes.

"I ordered that the women and children were to be held inviolate," Bakarat reminded his lieutenant in savage tones. "They are the only guarantee that the officers and crew of this ship will co-operate — and while we have that co-operation the women and children will not be harmed. If there is another incident such as this I will kill you myself. Do you understand?"

Zakaria stared up at him for almost a minute. Then he spat blood and slowly nodded.

Bakarat turned to Fraser. "This will

not happen again, Chief Officer, you have my word."

Fraser said nothing. It would all have to wait until that hour of retribution when he determined that they would pay for the dead man at his feet.

# 12

LATER that afternoon a Boeing 707 of Lufthansa Airlines touched down at London Airport. Among the passengers who disembarked was a tall, dark-haired man with serious eyes. His stride was stiff and somewhat self conscious but he passed through the airport controls with practised ease. Inspector Max Brenner was rated as the best marksman with both pistol and rifle that the West German *Bereitschaftpolizei* had yet produced, and he was also the Counter-Terror Section Head for Munich. Mark Nicolson was waiting for him with a car and they drove immediately to New Scotland Yard.

"What is it, Max?" Nicolson asked. "It must be important to bring you on a personal visit to London."

"Let it wait," Brenner smiled briefly,

"I'll explain when we meet the Co-ordinator, for I have the feeling that it will need three minds."

"You're too late for that," Nicolson told him. "Gwynne-Vaughan left London for Amsterdam only an hour ago. He wants to double-check with Dirk Helders on the security cover for the N.A.T.O. — Warsaw Pact talks. You must have come close to passing each other at twenty thousand feet."

Brenner's smile faded and he listened with the silence of a man who knew all the facts but was prepared to hear them reviewed just in case there was anything he had missed. They reached the Yard before Nicolson had concluded the breakdown of all the problems that faced them in Amsterdam. Then in the Counter-Terror office Brenner spread out the newspapers he had been carrying on Nicolson's desk.

"This could add to your headaches, Mark. I refer to the reports on the German freighter that was lost off Cape Finisterre in the early hours of this morning. The ship was called the *Rhineland* and she sank after an explosion in her engine room. The facts are all too brief and nothing is clearly known, but it appears that a supertanker called the *Monolith* answered her distress call and took some of the survivors aboard. The tanker is a British vessel, Mark — that is why it involves you."

Nicolson stared at him blankly. "Why should a tragedy at sea involve any of us?"

"As yet I am not sure, but I will try to explain." Brenner sat down and regarded him gravely. "Do you remember that six months ago we had rumours that a large terrorist gang had made plans to hi-jack a cross channel ferry. It was assumed that a Belgian ferry was to be the target because of Belgian plans to build an aircraft and missile plant for the Israelis and so for a few days all the Belgian Marine Services carried armed policemen."

Nicolson nodded slowly. "I remember it."

"Major Cassin believed that some of the Arab groups who were resident in Paris at that time had intended to take part in that attack," Brenner continued. "After the security clampdown on the channel ferries these groups began to disperse and one party of four men entered Germany. We were forewarned by the Paris office and so we continued to keep these men under observation. Their leader was a man named Zakaria and they made their way to Hamburg. There, after a few weeks, they signed ships articles as deckhands aboard a freighter."

Nicolson began to understand. "The *Rhineland*?" he hazarded softly.

It was Brenner's turn to nod. "The *Rhineland*," he agreed. "I could not think of any reason why they should be interested in an old cargo ship, but after the ferry scare I thought that it was best to put one of my own men aboard. I chose one of my best sergeants — a man who had just completed his two years training with the *Bereitschaftpolizei*. His name was Eric Weber, and he sailed as the *Rhineland*'s Third Officer."

"And now the *Rhineland* has met with disaster." Nicolson gazed down doubtfully at the limited news reports as he spoke.

"She made one uneventful voyage with the four Arabs on board," Brenner told him grimly. "After that Weber wanted to be withdrawn. He felt that it was a false alarm and that he was wasting his time. Now this happens!"

Nicolson was thinking hard. The French connection and the fact that Zakaria and his group had moved from Paris was ringing a far-off bell in his mind — and there was something else. The location Cape Finisterre disturbed him but he could not remember where it was. He asked Brenner.

"Cape Finisterre is off the north coast of Spain."

Brenner offered the information calmly

but it prompted Nicolson into immediate action. He shouted for Harry Stone and when his Detective Sergeant appeared he said briefly,

"Harry, get me the file with all our recent reports from Inspector Gaiani in Rome — and everything we have on the man Hasan Bakarat."

While they waited for Stone to fetch the reports Nicolson again looked to Max Brenner.

"Six months ago, there was another Arab group who withdrew from Paris to Rome," he explained. "Gaiani had some leads on them there, but then they made another hasty move to Madrid when one of their number was gunned down by the *Shinbeth*. The group leader in this case is a man named Bakarat and the last report we have indicates that his group is on the move somewhere in the northern part of Spain. What worries me now is the fact that Bakarat and your friend Zakaria must have been in Paris at about the same time. Whatever was planned there, it's a strong possibility that they planned it together."

Harry Stone brought in the relevant files and Nicolson and Brenner studied them in detail, trying to make sense out of the pieces they had and of all the unknown permutations at which they could only guess.

★ ★ ★

The long threatened storm finally exploded late in the afternoon when the *Monolith* was still only half way across the notorious Bay of Biscay. The black thunderclouds had built up out of the west until they had voraciously swallowed the last tattered shred of grey sky. The Atlantic seas had swelled from great rolling hills to careering mountains of grey-green and the winds had built up from gale force to a shrieking seventy miles per hour. The red fire of lightning split the black skies in a vivid devil's pitchfork and a rolling bellow of thunder precipitated a deluge. The *Monolith*, despite her mighty tonnage, began to pitch and roll, groaning and reeling beneath the mammoth hammer blows of the elements. The waves crashed over the green acres of her vast deck until it seemed that only the battered white island of the superstructure remained afloat.

Fraser was in command of the bridge but the moment that the storm erupted Armstrong rejoined him. Together they stood watch as the supertanker battled her way north, watching her speed and course and the radar screens, and sensitive to every stress and anguished movement of their belaboured monster. The storm became a hurricane, a frenzy of racing wind, lashing waves and torrents of rain. The transition from day to night was barely noticeable in the universal nightmare of howling darkness.

Eight bells rang and the weary helmsman and the two seamen who had struggled to help him at the wheel were replaced by the new watch. John Deverell reported to the bridge but Fraser and Armstrong both chose to remain. They knew that the hurricane would not relent until they had crossed the Bay.

Another hour passed. Bakarat and Takaaki were both present on the bridge but they had to allow Armstrong and his officers full freedom of movement to attend to the ship's needs. At first they had carefully monitored every scrap of conversation, but eventually they tired of jumping to attention every time there was a brief discussion on the ship's position or the possible duration of the storm. The passage of time had slowly blunted their alertness and the violent and constant motion was beginning to take its toll. An opportunity came when Fraser and Armstrong stood together over the radar screens, a brief moment when neither of their captors was within hearing.

"Bruce," Armstrong murmured, "I'm

going to order you below. I can take care of the ship with Mister Deverell, and it's just possible that you can take advantage of this foul weather."

Fraser did not look round. He knew that both Bakarat and Takaaki were showing white around the gills, which was a sure sign that they were feeling sea sickness. The outside roaring of the wind and rain muffled their words and he answered softly.

"What do you have in mind, sir?"

"Nothing suicidal, I don't want you to finish up like Mister Eldridge. At the same time I would like to know what these devils have in mind. So far they've told us nothing, but if we can find out what their intentions are for when we reach Rotterdam, then that in itself might prove to be a card in our favour."

"If they won't confide, how do we find out?"

"They brought a large suitcase aboard," Armstrong informed him quietly. "The one they call Yotaro has charge of it and somehow I don't believe that it contains his spare socks and clean underwear. It was important enough to be saved from the *Rhineland* and I've noticed that they handle it with extreme care. At the moment the suitcase is in my stateroom and Yotaro is with it, but he's greener than a poodle dog with worms so he shouldn't be too much of an obstacle."

"I'll give it a try," Fraser promised.

They moved apart and Armstrong waited another ten minutes before announcing his decision that Fraser should leave the bridge. For the benefit of the two terrorist leaders Fraser made a mild protest, causing Armstrong to point out aloud that one of them had to rest now in order to take command later. Bakarat accepted the argument and called to Farraj who was relaxing in the radio room.

"Farraj will escort you to your cabin, Chief Officer. There you can rest undisturbed." Bakarat paused and then issued a warning. "Remember that two of my men are now patrolling in the alleyways to ensure that officers who are not on duty do remain in their own quarters."

Fraser yawned. "I'll remember."

He went below with Farraj following a cautious three paces behind. The Chief Officer's suite on the *Monolith* consisted of a group of four rooms on the starboard side of B deck, a bedroom, bathroom, dayroom and an office. Fraser went inside and Farraj closed the door and locked it. Fraser listened for a moment as the Arab moved away and heard him pause for a few words of conversation with Hayashi and Shefik who were on patrol. Then there was silence as Farraj returned to the bridge.

Fraser poured himself a small whisky, injected a splash of soda water and then sat down to think. Given time he did not consider it beyond his capabilities to pick the lock on the door, but there was clearly no point in emerging into the alleyway outside only to find himself looking down the muzzles of two of the inevitable Schmeisser machine pistols. He had to think of something better than that and after a few moments he got up to prowl around the confines of his quarters in search of inspiration. There was no other door and there was only one window, and the latter looked out over a sheer drop to the sea-washed deck fifty feet below. The ship lurched heavily under another screaming thrust from the hurricane, but Fraser accepted that his choices were still limited to the door and the window. They were his only exits. He finished his whisky and by then he had made his decision.

He went into the bedroom to strip the bed and carefully knotted together four of the lightweight nylon sheets. Ideally he needed something to act as a grappling hook, but there was nothing to hand and finally he had to settle for a heavy glass ashtray to weight the end of his improvised rope. Then he returned to the dayroom and opened the window. The wind and the rain blasted inside with a deafening roar.

Fraser pushed his head and shoulders outside into the tormented darkness. A vertical waterfall of rain engulfed him and soaked him to the skin while a howling eighty mile wind tore at his face and clothes. He was blind, gasping immediately for breath, and the savage shock of that first contact with the storm forced him to momentarily withdraw. Then he gritted his teeth, filled his lungs and again thrust his head and shoulders out into the elements.

Below him the great waves crashed and thundered over the tanker's deck, pounding at the white cliff face of the island superstructure as though bent upon its collapse and destruction. White spume from the exploding wave tops reached up the full fifty feet for he could taste the salt in the rain that cascaded down his face. Down there was certain death in the black, snapping jaws of the monstrous seas, but Fraser had no intentions of climbing down. Instead he looked up to the deck rails of A deck almost invisible in the equally horrifying darkness above. He had to climb a short distance of approximately ten feet, which under these conditions was roughly equivalent to the last half mile of the north face of Everest.

There was no advantage in delay. The *Monolith* was being flung so violently from side to side that Fraser was in danger of losing his balance as he leaned out. He needed both hands to swing his rope and so he pulled up a heavy table and anchored himself inside the cabin with a hooked leg lock. Then, with his head and shoulders again thrust out into the howling hurricane, he endeavoured to throw the rope upwards. He made a dozen attempts and each time the powerful winds flung the knotted sheets right or left or drove them back into his face. His shoulders and arms ached and the whole crazy business seemed doomed and hopeless. Then with his thirteenth throw the ship reeled to port. The shrieking wind picked up the weighted end of the rope and carried it exactly where he wanted it, over the top rail of the deck above.

Fraser was gasping for breath again, blinded and choked by the downpour of rain crashing over his upturned face. Through slitted eyes he saw that the rope had caught and he waited desperately for the ship to make its next starboard roll. With a tortured moan the ship tilted and the force of gravity caused the weighted end of the rope to swing back between the top and centre rails. Fraser paid out the rope and the weight dropped down and all but smashed him in the face. He caught it and retreated thankfully inside the cabin where he discarded the glass ashtray and made both ends of the rope fast.

Fraser recovered his breath, flexed his arm and shoulder muscles, and after three minutes decided reluctantly that he was as fit as he would ever be. He went back to the window and heaved on the double rope. It held his weight. The nylon material was strong and he had confidence in his own knots, and so he put the rope and his own nerve and endurance to the final test. He hauled himself hand over hand, through the window and up the outside of the ship.

For a moment he stood on the lower edge of the window, standing upright and hanging on to the rope with the merciless winds lashing at his helpless body like giant bull whips wielded in fury by all the satanic lords of darkness. Below the huge seas boomed in paramount rage and reached for him with flailing white claws of bursting spray. The *Monolith* rolled to starboard and he swung away from her white flank, dangling like a lost puppet on an uncontrolled string.

The *Monolith* rolled again and he was slammed back against her side. He almost lost his grip and he knew that he could not survive many such blows. Neither could he last for too many seconds with the full force of the hurricane determined to break his grip and hurl him to his death. He began to haul himself up through the vertical cataract of rain and his ears were filled with the roaring of the water and the maniac screeching of the winds.

He was alive in hell, torn apart on a dozen racks that strove to separate him limb from limb. He couldn't breathe and every muscle cried in agony. The ship rolled and again he was spinning like a whipped top, and then again he was dashed cruelly against the cliff face of white steel. He felt as though every bone in his body was broken and every last gasp of air in his lungs was gone. His heart had panicked, starved of oxygen and racing like a pneumatic drill inside his chest. His fingers slipped on the wet nylon sheet and he knew his strength was failing. There was a rising black thunder inside his own brain that was swelling to equal the insane darkness that whirled around him. He knew that there were only seconds left before he gave up the unequal fight and fell.

As his fingers slipped he lunged desperately upward with one hand. The inside of his wrist hit a horizontal bar of steel, the palm of his hand slithered away from it and then his fingers hooked and held. He realized that he had reached the centre rail of the deck above and there was a spur of hope in him that held back the drowning wave of unconsciousness. He abandoned the sheet rope, transferring his other hand to the rail, and then he made the final effort on willpower alone. He pulled himself through the rails and then the *Monolith* mercifully tilted hard to port and helped to roll him on to the deck. He sprawled on his face and belly with one arm locked tightly round a stanchion and allowed the weight of the driving rods of rain to nail him down to the scrubbed boards.

He lay there for almost five minutes, oblivious to the elements, gulping down air into his starved lungs and praying for his heart to reduce its terrifying pounding to something near normal. While he lay flat and kept his arm lock on the stanchion he was relatively safe from being swept overboard and slowly he began to think out his next move. He was now on A deck, immediately below the bridge and only a few yards from the closed door of the Captain's stateroom. Behind that door was the mysterious suitcases he had determined to investigate — and one armed Japanese.

He had by-passed two guards and now he could only hope that Yotaro was as sick as Armstrong believed. He waited until the roll of the ship was pitching his momentum in the right direction and then he pushed himself up from the deck and made a frantic dive for the stateroom door. One crosswind puff from the hurricane could have lifted him out into space, but instead the wind slammed him squarely between the shoulder blades and drove him hard against the door.

He wrenched it open and stumbled inside.

The Captain's accommodation was a more spacious version of his own. He was in the wide dayroom and it was empty. To his left was Armstrong's office and ahead the door that led through to the bedroom and bathroom. Only a dead man could have failed to hear the opening of the outside door and the inward blast of the hurricane and so Fraser had no time to waste. Without hesitation he crashed forward through the second door into the bedroom.

Yotaro was struggling to get up from the bed. His face was ash grey, the same colour as his spiked hair, and he looked ill enough to die. There was a bowl of vomit on the bedside table and he had taken off his spectacles. However, his right hand was groping for his machine pistol and Fraser showed him no mercy. He grabbed the feebly moving Japanese by the collar of his jacket, heaved him up from the bed and then launched a pile-driving fist at the sagging jaw. Yotaro's head snapped back and hung limply.

For a moment Fraser believed and hoped that he had broken the man's neck, but then he decided that the slumped angle of the head was not that serious. As yet he had not become sufficiently cold blooded to kill an unconscious man and although the temptation was there he reluctantly let the Japanese fall back on to the bed.

He turned away and began to search for the vital suitcase.

★ ★ ★

Bruce Fraser was not the only man on the move. As the *Monolith* fought her way doggedly forward into the teeth of the hurricane another cautious figure moved furtively up the companionways from her lower decks. Eric Weber had also seen the slim thread of opportunity offered by the fearsome conditions that locked the ship in stupendous battle with the Atlantic. His own stomach felt queasy with the constant rolling, and so he had hopes that the terrorists who had even less seafaring experience would be feeling worse. In any case he could not foresee a better time and so he had decided upon a reconnaissance prowl to acquaint himself with the layout of the ship.

The blonde German had no positive course of action in mind and he had no intentions of trying to ascend to the level of the radio room and the bridge which he knew would be heavily guarded. Instead he hoped to gain a basic knowledge of the between decks, the run of the companionways and alleyways and the exact location of the saloon where the women and children were being held. The explanations and directions he had received from the Bo'sun might have been enough for any other man, but after what he considered to be his failure aboard the *Rhineland* Weber was incapable of sitting idle. He wanted his knowledge to be complete so that whenever a real opportunity arose for action he would be able to put it to full advantage.

He reached the top of a companionway and saw the double doors of the saloon down the corridor ahead. He risked going forward with his shoulders pressed against the wall and peered briefly through the glass panel in the nearest door. He saw Jackie Spencer lying on a blanket on the floor with the two little girls and five-year old Stephen pulled close around her. The other women and children were scattered wherever they could make themselves comfortable, some of them tired but awake and the others in shallow sleep. Three of the Arab deckhands from the *Rhineland* sat at the saloon tables with their heads cradled on their arms but with their machine pistols within inches of their fingers. Only Zakaria sat wide awake with his machine pistol resting across his knees.

Weber withdrew, wondering on the chances of attacking the saloon and taking the four Arabs by surprise. If he could devise a feasible plan he knew that he could rely upon Big Henry Elliot and enough determined seamen to back him up, but until he knew what the terrorists planned it was impossible to decide whether the potential consequences would be worth the risk. So far he only knew one side of the stakes and the lives of the children were terrible tokens with which to gamble. Any such raid would have to be a last-ditch effort, but at least he could discuss the possibility with the Bo'sun and the Chief Engineer when he returned below. In the meantime he decided to spy out the deck above.

He ascended the next companionway and explored with caution. Thirty seconds later he turned a corner of an alleyway and came face to face with Hayashi.

# 13

THERE is a limit to how finely you can split a second and still act first, but Weber moved with that infinitesimal paring of time in his favour. Hayashi was a hard, fanatical killer who prided himself with all the warrior qualities of a samurai, but he lost that hairline initiative because he recognized the Third Officer of the *Rhineland*. To the Japanese Eric Weber was a ghost from the dead, and although he recovered fast and brought his machine pistol up to fire, Weber's right foot was already flashing forward. The Schmeisser machine pistol was kicked out of Hayashi's hands and crashed to the deck. Then Weber followed up with a savage left hand jab to Hayashi's stomach and a right hand chop to the side of the falling man's neck.

Hayashi went down but he was not an easy man to beat. He rolled weakly, keeping his body moving to avoid another blow. Then his shoulder hit the bulkhead and he was forced to a stop. Weber knew that any second the Japanese would start shouting for help and so he aimed another murderous kick at Hayashi's jaw. The Japanese fooled him by lunging forward and grabbing at his swinging ankle before it gained momentum. Hayashi twisted and heaved and Weber was hurled in turn to the deck. They scrambled up together and then Hayashi reached both hands behind his left shoulder to grasp the hilt of his slung sword. He drew the weapon clear of its scabbard with one smooth jerk and then attacked with a wild, triumphant cry.

Weber ducked the first slashing sweep of the sword and then he ran. He turned the next corner of the alleyway with Hayashi two paces behind in hot pursuit and there he deliberately dropped to his knees and crouched low. Hayashi charged round the corner, tripped over Weber's shoulders and reeled past him with sword and arms flailing. Weber had hoped to topple the Japanese flat on his face, but although badly off balance Hayashi succeeded in keeping to his feet. Weber could not move in under the razor-edged blade of the sword, but while his opponent staggered he had a few seconds in which to look round for some means of defence. On the bulkhead wall there was a fire hose locker and above it a long handled fire axe. Weber wrenched the axe from its holding clips and sprang to meet Hayashi's next attack.

The heavy axe blade swept the descending sword aside. Hayashi sprang back, balanced on the balls of his feet, feinted and then lunged. Again Weber deflected the thrust with the fire axe. Hayashi peeled back his lips in a fanatic's grin and Weber knew that he had a fighting chance. The Japanese was too proud to cry for assistance and meant to stand alone to the death.

Again Hayashi closed in combat, his slit eyes blazing and his teeth still bared in that animal grin. Weber gave no ground, whirling the heavier axe with equal ferocity as they cut, hacked and parried. Weber barely felt the sting as the samurai blade slipped through his guard but suddenly there was blood pouring down his left arm. Hayashi drew back and laughed and in the same second Weber swung the axe with all his strength. The Japanese ducked his head and the heavy axe blade bit deep into solid woodwork. Too late Weber realized that he had struck an outer door, for the force of the blow crashed the door open and he was jerked out into the howling darkness where the hurricane raged.

Hayashi followed him out on to the open deck and the fight continued in the wind-lashed downpour of the night. Weber wrenched his weapon free and would have died as he turned if the strength of the hurricane had not forced Hayashi back against the deck

251

rails. The sword stroke that was meant to decapitate the young German failed to reach and Weber saw the bright tip of the blade slicing through the black curtain of rain only inches from his eyes.

The unpredictable rolling of the *Monolith* had handicapped both combatants from the beginning, but now on the wet, slippery deck it was a double hazard. Any move was suicidal against the shrieking power of the winds and Weber held fast with one hand to the wildly swinging door as he wielded the fire axe with the other. Hayashi also needed one hand to anchor himself to the ship's rail, and so they fought an insane one-handed duel while the infuriated elements sought to destroy them both.

Weber felt himself tiring rapidly. He was losing blood from the deep wound in his arm and the fire axe was proving heavier than the sword. Also Hayashi's anchor point was relatively stable while the open door was jerking Weber to and fro with every roll of the ship. Weber weighted the odds and then chanced everything on the will of the storm. He waited for the next roll of the deck to tilt him towards Hayashi and then he released his hold on the door and allowed his body to flail forward with the axe whirling up above his head and then down with one final, desperate blow. All his weight, the throw of the ship and the force of the hurricane were behind the fall of the axe. Hayashi screamed in the split second before the blade chopped through his collar bone, but the scream was ripped away by the winds. Weber grabbed at the rail to stop himself from flying overboard and hung there helpless with his last effort spent.

The hurricane continued to howl through the endless rainfall. Hayashi's body lolled on the deck, slithered away from the rail, and then was tumbled back again with the next starboard roll. The driving winds swept it out into the black night to be lost for ever under the mountainous waves of the thundering Atlantic, and within seconds the rain had washed the deck boards clean of the last great splash of blood.

Weber regained the interior of the ship, collected the machine pistol that Hayashi had dropped, and then stumbled below.

★ ★ ★

In Armstrong's cabin Bruce Fraser had located the large suitcase that the terrorists had taken such pains to bring aboard. It was locked, but he searched the unconscious Yotaro and found a bundle of keys in one of the little man's pockets. One key fitted the suitcase and Fraser opened it with care. He had no preconceived expectations and so he was baffled by what he saw. The suitcase was simply an outer leather camouflage which fitted exactly over a polished steel container built to the same dimensions. There was no obvious way into the steel casing, but built into the flat surface was an inset control panel that included a radial glass dial and three small tuning knobs.

Fraser knelt on the cabin floor and stared down at his discovery. He was still soaking wet and the rain leaking from his clothes was ruining the expensive carpet, but now for the first time he shivered and felt cold. The control panel suggested some kind of electronic equipment, and he didn't dare to hope that it was an obscene model of an outsize transistor radio. His commonsense and the ice-winged butterflies crawling in his gut told him that it had to be a bomb.

Slowly Fraser realized that he was not surprised. He remembered the total destruction of the *Rhineland* and in the back of his mind the fear had always been present that a similar ending could be the fate of the *Monolith*. Almost certainly the thought had been in Armstrong's mind too. Until now neither of them had been prepared to let that fearsome thought come forward for open consideration, but now they had no choice.

Fraser closed the suitcase and thought for a moment. A whirl of horrific images filled his brain and through them all there was one sharp clarion call for action. The device in his hands, coupled with the awesome fire potential of the *Monolith*'s quarter-of-a-million ton cargo of inflammable crude oil, would be enough to blow them all to hell and beyond a dozen times over. Every second that it remained on board the ship would be a continuing nightmare and he had to get rid of it.

The best place for such lethal hardware was the bottom of the sea, but there were problems that precluded the simple act of dumping it overboard. Fraser knew that any object thrown over the side in a storm was liable to be hurled right back in his face by the wind and even in calm weather there would still be that long drop from the tanker's deck to the surface of the waves. The bomb could explode upon impact and still be close enough to cause disaster.

Fraser sweated but there was only one immediate answer. Before it could be jettisoned the suitcase had to be removed out of reach of the terrorists. At the very least he had to smuggle it below and conceal it where it could not be found and used. He could insist to Bakarat that it had been thrown over the side and then let them do their worst.

He re-locked the case prior to carrying it below and as he turned the key he heard a faint sound. The door to the dayroom behind him and the door to the exposed deck beyond were both still open. He could hear the outer door swinging on its hinges as it was buffetted by the wind and rain, but the muffled click that had penetrated through the general blur of storm noise could only have been the opening of the door from the dayroom to Armstrong's office. Through the office and up a short companionway was the direct route to the bridge.

Fraser turned swiftly on one knee as Koiso Takaaki appeared in the bedroom doorway. There was rage in the pebble eyes behind the glittering spectacles and Takaaki's machine pistol was levelled in his hands. Fraser instinctively lifted the suitcase as a shield as he rose to his feet and the sudden panic expression on Takaaki's face told him that the Japanese would not fire. Fraser took a blind chance and threw the suitcase with all his strength. Takaaki caught it with one hand and clutched it tightly to his chest as he staggered back under the weight. His face was white with fear and he dropped his machine pistol as he endeavoured to prevent the suitcase from crashing to the deck.

Fraser dived for the foot of the bed where he had placed Yotaro's machine pistol ready to hand. His fingers closed over the black steel but in the same second the barrel of another weapon smashed down over his knuckles. His hand was trapped and bloodied between the two gun muzzles and as he rolled on to his back to face Takaaki's companion a steel-shod boot slammed into his crotch. Fraser made another effort to close his pain-filled fingers around Yotaro's machine pistol but then it was hooked spinning out of his reach.

"I should kill you, Chief Officer," Hasan Bakarat spat the words into his face. "You are a dangerous fool and I should kill you quickly. Give me one good reason why I should not finish this business and kill you now?"

Fraser stared at him and realized that he was only a milligram of finger pressure away from death. There was only one answer and he hung his life on it as he struggled to keep his tone calm and reasonable.

"You won't kill me because you need me, Captain Armstrong has already spent the last ten hours on the bridge. There's another ten to go before we clear the Bay and can hope to get out of this hurricane, and then we've got twenty-four hours of moving up the most congested sea lanes in the world. At some stage the Captain has to sleep while I take over."

Bakarat hesitated. "When it becomes necessary the Second Officer can take over from the Captain."

"Not in a hurricane," Fraser told him bluntly. "And not in waters where there is a constant collision risk and navigation has to be one hundred per cent accurate. This isn't a penny yacht, Bakarat, it's one of the biggest ships you'll find on any ocean. She doesn't leave any room for navigational errors!"

Bakarat was trembling. His eyes burned, his mouth twitched, and his finger ached on the trigger. There was a part of him that was deaf and blind to reason that wanted to kill this man now. At the same time the fact remained that the *Monolith* had to reach the Rotterdam Europort on schedule and there was undeniable truth in Fraser's words. With an exhausted Captain and one inexperienced junior officer the gargantuan supertanker would be wide open to any natural misfortune.

While Bakarat hovered between reason and desire Takaaki lowered the suitcase carefully to the ground. The Japanese picked up his machine pistol and the key that Fraser had dropped. He made sure that Bakarat had Fraser covered and then he knelt to open up the suitcase and peer carefully at the control panel inside.

"The warhead appears to be undamaged," he said with relief. He got up and crossed to the bed. "And Yotaro is alive. As soon as he recovers he will make a proper examination to be sure."

"A warhead?" For the moment Fraser forgot Bakarat and stared at the Japanese. "What exactly is that thing?"

Takaaki stared at him coldly and then decided that the harm was done and that there was a cruel pleasure to be derived from explaining what remained.

"This thing, Chief Officer, is the

warhead from a guided surface to air missile. Normally it requires a twenty-five foot rocket with boosters, an electronic guidance control system and target-seeking radar to launch it on its way at two-thousand-five-hundred miles per hour. We, or rather our good friend Yotaro, have dispensed with all that. The components of the warhead itself have simply been repositioned slightly so that it can fit into these more convenient dimensions, and everything else has been replaced by a pre-set timing control which occupies relatively negative space."

Fraser felt as though a coating of frost had formed around his heart and along his spine.

"To what purpose?" he asked slowly.

"To strike a blow for Palestine!"

Bakarat cried the words with fierce passion and with them his decision was made. He stepped away from Fraser and with a physical effort relaxed his finger on the trigger of his machine pistol.

"Again you will live, Chief Officer, because as you so rightly perceive we still need you. But it is time for us to understand each other. To comprehend the futility of your continued resistance it is necessary for you to understand me."

Bakarat paused to control the tremor in his voice and then continued harshly: "When I first came to Europe the target for my group was the Q.E.2. You may remember that the liner carried twelve hundred filthy rich Jews to Israel to celebrate the twenty-fifth anniversary of the bandit state that occupies Palestine — my country! Our plan was to attach magnetic mines to the ship's hull but she was too closely guarded, and when we learned that Royal Navy frogmen were diving to search for such mines we knew that our plan was hopeless and had to be abandoned.

"We laid more plans and our second target was to have been a cross channel ferry. Somehow that plan leaked and again we were foiled when the Western security forces put a close guard on all the cross channel ports.

"So we withdrew to plan a third time, and it was then that we learned that the Japanese Red Star Army had acquired a missile warhead which they were willing to place at our disposal. Together we planned this combined operation, and this time we shall not fail! The operation will succeed because it has reached the stage where neither you nor anyone else can stop us."

There was silence as Bakarat reached the end of his outburst. He paused for breath and Takaaki had nothing to add. Fraser waited for a moment and then risked a quiet question.

"Why, Bakarat? Why does your operation have to succeed?"

Bakarat stared at him bitterly. "If you can ask that it means that you have never seen a Palestine refugee camp. You think that I am some kind of monster because I threaten your ship and the handful of women and children on board — but do you know how many millions of women and children are rotting and dying in the refugee camps? Is it beyond your imagination to picture the plight of a nation of people who are homeless and damned? Can you know anything of the misery and despair, the poverty and degradation of those camps? No, Chief Officer, you know nothing — and the terrible thing is that like the rest of the world you do not even want to know!"

"But does this help?" Fraser asked. "The murder of the *Rhineland*, whatever you have planned for the *Monolith*, Munich and the airport massacres, the embassy attacks and the sky-jackings and all the rest of it. Does any of it really help the people in those camps?"

"Does it matter now?" Bakarat shrugged and for a moment Fraser sensed the empty corrosion of hate and bitterness that had eaten away the Arab's soul. "Once we hoped that our terrorist attacks would draw world attention to the Palestine problem, and lead to a just solution. Now we know that no matter what happens the world does not care. The politicians of the world do not give a damn for the Palestine people. Their answer is not justice for Palestine, but simply to crush down her sons who refuse to sit in the camps and rot.

"So now our terrorism is the defiance of pure desperation. Terror for its own sake. All that we can do is fight and vow — and we vow that while there is no justice for Palestine, there will be no peace for the world!"

# 14

BAKARAT was taking no more chances. He couldn't spare a man to guard Fraser's quarters and so they all returned to the bridge where Fraser was obliged to get what sleep he could on the radio room floor. There he was under the alert eye of Odusu who was monitoring all radio messages.

Fraser slept for four hours, despite the hard discomfort and the tumultuous motion of the ship. The sound of eight bells ringing the end of the midnight watch awakened him and he saw that Derek Holbrook had now replaced Alan Spencer as the duty Radio Officer. Under the threat of Odusu's machine pistol Holbrook sat well back from his transmitters with his headphones lying on the table just out of reach. If anything came through Odusu listened to every word. Weather reports were still essential to the *Monolith* and all incoming calls had to be acknowledged to allay the suspicions of the outside world. The Radio Officers were permitted to do that much and no more. Bakarat had decreed that the first man who tried to send an unauthorized message out would be shot as an example to the others.

Fraser stood up carefully, making sure that he gave Odusu no cause for alarm.

"Good morning, Mister Holbrook," he said calmly. And then to Odusu: "I have to report to the bridge."

The Japanese was sitting at a safe distance with his back to the wall. He got up from his chair with his machine pistol still levelled and moved sideways to the door. He called a warning to the bridge and then signed to Fraser to pass.

They had sailed through the storm centre of the hurricane, but the bad weather still persisted with gale force winds, non-stop rain and warlike seas. Armstrong stood by the helmsman looking raw-eyed and weary. When he saw Fraser return he welcomed him with a smile. Then he dismissed his Second Officer who was standing radar watch with orders to return to take the forenoon watch at eight a.m. John Deverell hesitated but then went below to sleep.

Fraser noted that Takaaki and Farraj were missing, presumably resting while Bakarat and Shefik stood guard. Like the ship's officers the terrorists also needed to take a few minimum hours of sleep before the *Monolith* began its last-lap haul up the English Channel.

The hours of the morning watch dragged away as the supertanker slogged through the last sea miles of the tempestuous Bay of Biscay. By seven a.m. she was rounding the Isle of Ushant off the north west coast of France, a vast quarter circle turn that took two hours before the titanic bows were steady on their new course north east by east into the mouth of the Channel. By then Deverell had returned, but Armstrong waited another hour until the ship was safe behind the sheltering land mass of Brittany which now held back the worst of the storm still raging in the Bay. Then the Captain handed over his command to Fraser and went below to collapse into an exhausted sleep.

The darkness had given way to a reluctant dawn of dreary grey skies. The rain abated but the seas were tireless. The full fury of the Atlantic was behind them but still the waves were hostile. Spray and rain still blurred most of the tanker's long green deck.

Takaaki and Farraj reappeared and Bakarat and Shefik went below. Yotaro, deathly pale but recovered and capable replaced Odusu. A steward brought plates of sandwiches and pots of hot coffee on to the bridge. They all ate standing upright, the terrorists maintaining their wary watch on the officers and crew, Deverell keeping eternal vigilance over the radar screens, and Fraser standing by the helmsman as the ship ploughed its mighty furrow through the waves.

Unexpectedly Odusu came back to the bridge. His smooth face was worried and he conversed briefly with Takaaki. Fraser looked at them curiously but they spoke in Japanese which was beyond his understanding. Takaaki glared back at him coldly and then glanced to Farraj.

"Stand guard alone," he said briefly. "If either officer tries anything foolish, kill him."

Farraj stared blankly but then he put aside his sandwich and nodded. He moved so that he could cover both Fraser and Deverell with his machine pistol and then Takaaki and Odusu left the bridge.

Fraser wondered what was happening and whether this sudden reduction of terrorist strength could be turned to advantage. He toyed with the idea of throwing his scalding cup of coffee into the dark, bullfrog face, but a sideways glance told him that Farraj was prepared. He drank the coffee slowly, still thinking, but only five minutes passed before Odusu and Takaaki were back again with Bakarat beside them.

The fact that his few brief hours of sleep had been interrupted was enough to make Bakarat irritable, but there was more than mere irritation in his eyes. He was angry and he stopped squarely in front of Fraser.

"What has happened to Hayashi?" he demanded.

"Hayashi?" Fraser repeated the name and looked blank.

Bakarat's eyes held menace and his tone was accusing.

"One of Takaaki's men is missing. We have searched the upper part of the ship and cannot find him."

Fraser shrugged. "So what? Why come to me?"

"Because Hayashi was on patrol last night and for a brief period you were free. Hayashi has not been seen since that time. If he has vanished then you may be responsible!"

"I climbed out of my cabin window," Fraser reminded him. "I climbed up to the Captain's stateroom and you caught me inside. I didn't pass through the interior of the ship and I didn't encounter any of your guards."

"Then where is Hayashi?"

Again Fraser shrugged. "How should I know? There was a hurricane last night. If he was fool enough to go out on to an exposed deck he was probably swept over the side."

"Hayashi would not be such a fool," Takaaki exploded. "I knew him like a brother."

"Then think up your own explanations," Fraser told him. "It's not my problem."

"You are lying, Chief Officer," Bakarat's eyes blazed like black coals. "You must know something."

They stared at each other, Fraser cool and curious and Bakarat firmly disbelieving his innocence, and then they were interrupted. Derek Holbrook emerged from the radio room with a message sheet in his hand and Yotaro following close behind. Yotaro spoke quickly to Takaaki.

"What is it, Mister Holbrook?" Fraser asked.

"A message from Hamburg, sir," Holbrook said quietly. "It's from the owners of the *Rhineland*. They say that they've been trying to reach us for the past twenty-four hours, but that they haven't been able to make contact because of the storm. They request a more explicit account of the loss of the *Rhineland*, sir, plus the names of the survivors we have on board. It seems that there are a lot of worried relatives in Hamburg, especially the Captain's wife."

Bakarat tightened his mouth, frowning as he considered this new difficulty. Then he looked to Farraj.

"Go down to the saloon and tell Zakaria that he is needed on the bridge. He should be able to give us enough names to make up a satisfactory list."

Farraj nodded and hurried away.

Bakarat stared down doubtfully at the message sheet he had taken from Holbrook's uncertain hand, and the disappearance of Hayashi was temporarily forgotten.

★ ★ ★

The telephone rang in the Counter-Terror office in New Scotland Yard. Harry Stone picked it up, listened for a moment and then offered it across the desk to Mark Nicolson.

"It's from Madrid, sir," he said briefly. "Police Captain Ramondez asking for Sir Alexander."

Nicolson felt suddenly optimistic as he took the phone. He introduced himself and explained that the Co-ordinator was still in Holland. Ramondez sounded friendly, although his English was slow and careful, and after establishing that Nicolson knew the full nature of Gwynne-Vaughan's enquiries he offered his information.

"There are some small points that may interest you, Superintendent, although I am not sure how much they will help. The *Guardia Civil* in Corrunna Province have discovered two motor cars abandoned near the Atlantic coast just south of Cape Finisterre. One was a Peugeot and the other a Mercedes. Through the licence plates we have discovered that both vehicles were hired. The Peugeot we have traced to a firm in Zaragoza. It was hired by a tall man of Arab nationality who fits the description I have of the man Hasan Bakarat. The name on the passport he showed when the car was hired was different, but these people have any number of forged passports."

"And the second car?" Nicolson queried.

"The Mercedes was hired from a car firm in Madrid by two Japanese. They gave the names Odusu and Yotaro, but again these names could be true or false."

Nicolson was frowning. A Japanese involvement was an unexpected twist but something that was not impossible in the present political climate. There had been combined operations before. He said slowly,

"Are you sure that there is a connection between the two cars?"

"They were abandoned within a few miles of each other," Ramondez assured him. "And there is another coincidence that may be of interest to you. The Peugeot was found in a copse of trees only half a mile from a small fishing village where one of the fishing boats has been reported missing. The boat in question is called the *Beatriz*. Her owner was a man named Giovanni Vasquez. The village people say that Vasquez was approached by two Japanese who wanted to accompany him on a fishing trip. The Japanese said that they were magazine writers. The *Beatriz* sailed with Vasquez and his son Luis, and presumably the two Japanese on board, and she has not been seen since."

"You say presumably — didn't anyone see them go aboard?"

"I am told that it was a filthy night, black and raining. Also it is a small village. The village people were all indoors."

"Then it is possible that our three Arabs from the Peugeot also went on board the *Beatriz* with the Japanese?"

Juan Ramondez was silent for a moment but then he admitted cautiously; "It is possible."

"When did this happen?" Nicolson asked. "When did the *Beatriz* sail?"

There was a faint rustle of papers as Ramondez checked his notes.

"Two nights ago," Ramondez said. "About three hours before midnight."

Nicolson's handsome face became grim, for it was on that night that the *Rhineland* had been lost in the same seas.

After Nicolson had thanked Juan Ramondez warmly for his help he rang off and then replayed the tape of their conversation to Harry Stone. Again they reviewed every fact and fragment that they had and one point slowly became clear. As yet they did not know how the threads of their investigation knotted together, but every thread led unmistakably to the same pin-point area of the Atlantic Ocean.

"What do we have on this tanker that picked up the survivors from the *Rhineland*?" Nicolson asked at last.

"I spoke to a representative of the shipping company that owns her yesterday." Stone consulted his notebook. "The *Monolith* is one of these new supertankers, she weighs two-hundred-and fifty-thousand tons and she's due to reach the Europort oil terminal at Rotterdam at noon tomorrow."

"She's big," Nicolson murmured thoughtfully. "And we are expecting something big to hit Holland."

"But according to the company spokesman there's nothing to indicate that there is anything wrong. Making allowances for bad weather interference the *Monolith* is still transmitting and receiving radio messages as normal."

"How many crew does she carry?"

"Just over fifty," Stone consulted his notebook again. "I have got a complete list here. Her Captain is a man named Hugh Armstrong, he's got a lifetime of experience at sea and he's considered by the company to be one-hundred percent capable." Stone paused and then added. "Oh, and some of the officers have their wives on board. The Merchant Navy sounds pretty domesticated these days. I've got a list of five wives and six children all under school age."

Nicolson snapped to attention. "Five women and six kids — Christ, Harry! Think what perfect hostages they would make if a terrorist group has managed get on board!"

Stone hesitated for a moment and then said slowly. "There's one way to check it out, sir. By now the *Monolith* should be entering the English Channel. The Navy have helicopter stations in Cornwall and the tanker is easily within their range. We could land a dozen helicopters on a deck that size."

"But what if our fears prove right, Harry? What happens if that tanker is under terrorist control and they're using those women and children as human shields?"

Stone's blunt face registered dismay. "I don't know, sir."

"Neither do I," Nicolson admitted grimly. "That's why we have to know what's happening on that ship before we go charging in with a hairy bunch of airborne coppers and commandos."

★ ★ ★

At noon the telephone rang again. Nicolson picked it up quickly, hoping for more positive news from Ramondez. However, this time the call was from Max Brenner who had returned to Munich.

"Mark, I fear the worst," Brenner said distinctly. "This morning I contacted a director of the shipping company that owned the *Rhineland*. At my request the company transmitted a radio message to the *Monolith* asking for more information on the loss of their vessel and also for a list of survivors. At my instigation the message to the *Monolith* also carried a supposed enquiry from the wife of Captain Schreiber, the master of the *Rhineland*. The reply that was radioed back was very convincing and the list of survivors had the name of Captain Schreiber at the top. There was also a message from Captain Schreiber assuring his wife that he was safe and well and that he would be with her soon."

Brenner paused. Nicolson guessed the rest but he waited for Brenner to finish.

"Mark, there is no Frau Schreiber — she died of a heart attack seven years ago. Therefore the message that

282

was received from the *Monolith* is an invention. There is definitely something very wrong on board your tanker!"

"Thanks, Max," Nicolson said quietly. "I'll inform the Co-ordinator and let you know about anything that develops."

He put the phone down and looked at Harry Stone.

"Now we know."

# 15

THE *Monolith*'s slow passage through the congested waters of the English Channel took twenty-four hours. The weather cleared and the sea was comparatively calm, but as the Channel narrowed Armstrong and Fraser remained permanently on the bridge. For most of the time John Deverell watched the radar screens, keeping a constant track of the numerous other vessels that now registered within their immediate area. Darkness fell as they entered the Straits of Dover and near midnight they crossed the busy sea lane between Dover and Calais.

Bakarat waited two more hours, until they were clear of the bottleneck and into the safer and widening waters of the North Sea. Then he conferred with Takaaki and they approached the

Captain and Fraser.

"It is time," Bakarat said simply. "We want all our preparations made before dawn. You will continue to command the bridge, Captain. You, Chief Officer, will accompany us."

"Time for what?" Armstrong demanded sharply. "What preparations?"

"Watch from the bridge and you will see."

Bakarat was too weary to show anger at Armstrong's tone. He motioned to Farraj and Shefik to take over and then gave Fraser an almost gentle prod with the muzzle of his machine pistol. Fraser hesitated but then decided that it would neither prove nor solve anything to argue. He turned and preceded the two terrorist leaders as they left the bridge.

On Bakarat's order he led the way to the Captain's stateroom. The terrorists had been taking it in turn to rest there with the care of the missile warhead as their only responsibility. Odusu was there now and he rolled off the bed with his machine pistol levelled as Fraser entered. He saw Bakarat and Takaaki and relaxed and then Bakarat sent him to relieve Yotaro in the radio room.

When Yotaro had joined them Bakarat indicated the deadly suitcase and smiled ironically at Fraser.

"You have a privilege, Chief Officer — you may carry the warhead down to the main deck."

Fraser saw no option and reluctantly picked up the suitcase. He led the small procession down through the interior of the ship until they finally emerged on the vast green deck at the base of the island superstructure. Here the night air was cool with a tang of the sea. The *Monolith* was rolling gently beneath a few half-masked stars that glittered faintly through the black shroud of darkness.

Takaaki pushed past Fraser and took the lead, following the line of massive steel pipelines that ran along the centre of the deck. At intervals there were branching pipelines leading out at right angles to connect up to the individual cargo tanks, and half way along the deck were the transverse pipelines that would be coupled up to dockside connections when the crude oil was to be pumped aboard or ashore.

Takaaki stopped just before the barrier of transverse pipelines, and immediately beside the oiltight access hatch to the central cargo tank.

"This will do," he decided.

Bakarat signed to Fraser to set the suitcase down. Yotaro opened it up on the deck and knelt reverently over the exposed warhead. He checked his wristwatch and then adjusted the setting of the radial dial on the control panel. Then he turned a switch and the whole panel glowed dimly red. Yotaro smiled with satisfaction and then spoke to Takaaki in Japanese.

"We need a length of rope," Takaaki translated. "And a sheet of oilproof covering."

"The Bo'sun's store locker is in the bows," Bakarat said knowledgeably. "You will open it, Chief Officer, and get what we need — also any tools nescessary to open this hatch."

Under the threat of the machine pistol Fraser couldn't refuse. He swallowed his frustration and went forward with Bakarat keeping a safe distance at his heels. The Bo'sun's locker was situated in the raised forepeak and as he opened it Fraser hoped that Bakarat would follow him into the darkness inside. He knew exactly where to lay his hand on the nearest marlinespike and all he asked was one chance to use it. However, Bakarat stayed well back from the doorway.

"Switch on the light," the tall Arab warned grimly. "I want to see exactly what you are doing in there."

Fraser cursed inwardly. He was half way through the door but he stopped and switched on the electric light. Bakarat came closer behind him and surveyed the interior of the locker room over his shoulder. The machine pistol nudged Fraser's spine.

"That rope will do, and the folded tarpaulin. And bring a hammer to knock off the clamps on the access hatch."

Fraser collected the items indicated and then turned. Bakarat withdrew backwards and motioned him out on to the open deck again. The hammer in his hand would be equally as effective as a marlinespike, but Fraser knew that he would be cut down the moment that he tried to use it. He led the way slowly back to where Takaaki and Yotaro waited.

The two Japanese took the tarpaulin and spread it open on the deck. Yotaro had already closed up the suitcase that contained the primed missile and the case was laid in the centre of the tarpaulin. Carefully the tarpaulin was folded back over the suitcase to make a tightly sealed and oilproof package and then it was secured with one end of the rope.

"Open the hatch," Bakarat ordered. Fraser almost choked with baffled fury. He struck off the clamps holding the hatch cover with savage force and then heaved the cover open. The stink of the heavy crude oil rose up in swirls of explosive vapour. One naked match flame now would be enough to ignite the released fumes and blow them all to glory, but Takaaki and Yotaro were still smiling as they lowered their million times more powerful missile into the open manhole. The missile sank beneath the black surface of the oil and after some fifteen feet of the rope had been paid out Takaaki secured it to the underside of the hatch cover.

"This is an idea we gleaned from the I.R.A.," Bakarat informed Fraser calmly. "In Belfast they suspended a gelignite charge protected by a plastic bag inside a petrol tanker. We have elaborated on their crude efforts and planned on what might be termed a *Monolithic* scale." He laughed at his own joke. "We shall achieve incomparably more than they have ever dreamed."

★ ★ ★

They returned to the bridge where Armstrong waited. The Captain had watched all their movements and had no need to ask what was intended. He faced Bakarat and demanded bluntly:

"When is that thing due to explode?"

"We are due to reach the Europort oil terminal at noon," Bakarat answered. "Therefore the device has been timed to explode one hour later. If you reach port on schedule, Captain, you will have sixty minutes to evacuate your crew and clear the surrounding area. We, of course, will not leave the ship until the last possible moment."

"Sixty minutes isn't enough!" Armstrong rasped harshly. "If I'm to alert the port authorities and get the whole area cleared there just isn't enough time."

"It is all the time we are prepared to give."

Armstrong glared into the hawk eyes. He clenched both fists but then had to let them fall back helplessly to his sides.

"You'll tear my ship apart and create a holocaust that will be equal to a nuclear explosion. Why, man? For God's sake why?"

"To disrupt the peace talks that are being held in Amsterdam between the countries of N.A.T.O. and the Warsaw Pact," Bakarat explained simply. "They hope to reach agreement on scaling down the vast standing armies and military forces they have built up in Europe. We do not want that peace conference to succeed. Holland is a small country and a major disaster on this scale at the Europort will throw all of her police and security forces into confusion. The explosion will be heard in Amsterdam, and in that confusion there will be trained assassination teams ready to strike at the conference delegations. There will be no peace for Europe. It will be murder for the sake of murder! Terror for the sake of terror! And if you ask me why, Captain Armstrong, then I must answer that it is because I am a Palestine Arab — and for my people there is nothing left!"

There was a long silence. Armstrong saw that where only despair and desperation remained, reason could not prevail. Finally he drew a deep breath and squared his shoulders.

"Mister Bakarat, I will not co-operate. The *Monolith* will not turn into the Rotterdam Europort. Instead she will maintain a straight course out into the North Sea."

The cruel lips narrowed and Bakarat nodded slowly as though he had expected no less.

"Think first, Captain. If you refuse, you must die. I have no doubt that the Chief Officer will follow your heroic example and he too will die. But your Second Officer will not die."

Bakarat paused to look at John Deverell and then he turned back to Armstrong and Fraser.

"Remember that I succeeded once before by putting pressure on one of your junior officers. Perhaps your Second Officer will prove stronger than the unfortunate Mister Eldridge, but he will be forced to witness greater horrors than the beheading of one seaman. First he will watch the execution of his Captain. Then the execution of his Chief Officer. Then I shall have the women brought to the bridge, and if necessary the children!" Bakarat's eyes blazed wildly. "Remember that one of those women is the Second Officer's wife! How many times do you think he could watch the swing of a samurai sword before he breaks and becomes obedient to my will?"

Deverell was staring at them from his position by the radar screens. His gaze was steady but his face was bloodless and he had nothing to say.

Bakarat meant every word and Armstrong knew that he could not delegate such a merciless responsibility.

★ ★ ★

The last dawn broke over the eastern sky, bringing an unexpectedly bright day with blue skies over the long grey seas. The seagulls, a sure promise of land, wheeled around the *Monolith* on clean white wings, but their cheerful cries of homecoming were a grim mockery. Ostende and the last miles of the Belgian coastline passed beyond the horizon to starboard, and when eight bells rang for the end of the morning watch the supertanker was steaming north east off the deltas of the Dutch coast.

On the bridge Fraser and Armstrong racked their brains in search of some means of escape from the fiery catastrophe that awaited them but they could see no hope.

In the saloon Zakaria and his group

were tense and constantly alert. The children were now miserable and the baby cried, and the nerves of the five women were frayed almost to breaking point. There were no more attempts to amuse the little ones and no one had tasted food since the evening before. The women all knew that it was only the danger to themselves that prevented the officers and crew from putting up a fight and so their fears had become tinged with guilt and a certain sense of responsibility.

Elizabeth Fergusson felt that she ought to do something, but time was running out and she did not know what.

Sue Deverell was plagued by the same feeling. She had the beginning of an idea but there was no way to discuss it with Elizabeth or the others because their guards had forbidden any whispering. They could speak aloud or be quiet, which meant inevitably the increased strain of prolonged silence.

Sue's idea was quite simply to seduce

Zakaria. She knew the tall Arab was still lustful, but she also knew that she was a strong woman and that no man could make love with a machine pistol in his hands. If she could tempt him and went willingly to a cabin, then perhaps there would be a chance to claw at his eyes at the right moment. If she could blind him and get the gun — Her thoughts trailed off there because she did not know what she could do next.

However, it would be a start. She stopped sitting with her knees held prudently together and allowed her skirt to ride up over her lovely thighs. Zakaria noticed and began to stare. Sue wanted to flinch from his dark eyes, but instead she steeled herself to risk a half-teasing smile, the kind of smile that had caused the young officers to compete for her company.

Immediately she sensed a rising resentment from Jackie and Jane. It was something she had not calculated and she felt suddenly ashamed. She realized that the other women either misunderstood her intentions completely, or they suspected her ruse and feared that she might provoke an incident which would ultimately harm the children.

For a moment Sue's brain was a tumult of conflicting urges and emotions, but then Zakaria resolved the issue by deliberately looking away. Sue realized that no matter what she decided she had lost, because Zakaria was taking no more chances of incurring Bakarat's wrath.

Sue pulled down her skirt but the damage was done. The other women remained hostile and the tension had increased. Soon they would all be on the brink of screaming hysteria.

★ ★ ★

The *Monolith* was barely rolling as she thrust her majestic way through the calm seas. It was a fine blue April morning with no trace of cloud. The hurricane was only a memory but the nightmare continued.

★ ★ ★

In the crew's mess Eric Weber argued with Big Henry Elliot. Hayashi's machine pistol lay on the table between them and Weber formed endless plans for its use. All were suicidal and the Bo'sun counselled patience. They didn't know fully what was happening and Elliot feared that any rash move could be a mistake.

★ ★ ★

On the bridge Armstrong gave the order for speed on the great sixty-ton propeller to be decreased. Slowly the *Monolith* began to lose way. By eleven a.m. her speed had been cut by half and the silver glitter of the great oil refineries of the Europort showed on the horizon.

Armstrong looked haggard, his eyes

299

sunken beneath the fierce brows, his cheeks cavernous and his mouth a thin-lipped line. Bruce Fraser couldn't see his own face but he knew that his own appearance could be no better.

★ ★ ★

Hasan Bakarat waited like a man possessed, a prophet of fury whose will was about to be fulfilled in a cataclysm of fire. Madness was his only heritage and for a moment he almost dared to believe that out of the destruction and the slaughter a new Palestine Nation might one day be permitted to rise like the phoenix from the refugee camps and the ashes.

The oil refineries, the largest in Europe, the bright silver storage tanks gleaming in the sunshine, the harbour basins and the long jetties of the great Europort, all began to take definite shape. The *Monolith* slowed to a crawl, a vulnerable dinosaur composed of steel and oil and no longer in control of her own destiny.

The officers and terrorists on the bridge saw the white pilot boat speeding out to meet them with the Dutch flag fluttering bravely in the bows. Armstrong hesitated but then ordered the two seamen on watch to go down to the main deck and cast out the rope ladder to help the pilot aboard. Bakarat advised the two sailors against conveying any warnings and then allowed them to pass.

The white motor launch disappeared under the huge black overhang of the hull. Those on the bridge saw the two seamen reach the deck and throw out the rope ladder and then they watched and waited while the pilot made the long climb up to the rails. Finally a man clambered into view, but then Bakarat stiffened as he saw that the pilot was not alone. Three men climbed on to the *Monolith*'s deck and paused there to catch their breath.

"Who are the others?" Bakarat

demanded harshly.

Armstrong and Fraser stared down at the deck below, but neither of them recognized the two additional faces. Fraser shrugged but Armstrong made a guess.

"Dock officials, I suppose."

Bakarat frowned but he saw no reason to panic. Three men or one, it made no real difference. He had decided against another tiresome conflict of wills and so he did not intend to reveal the presence of himself and his men to the pilot until the *Monolith* was actually alongside the jetty head. He issued more dire warnings to Armstrong and Fraser and then ordered his men to conceal themselves in pre-planned positions.

★ ★ ★

When the two seamen returned with the Dutch Pilot and his two companions there was nothing to indicate that Captain Hugh Armstrong was not in undisputed command of his own ship. The pilot was a tubby little man named Van Eerden who was well known to both Armstrong and Fraser. He climbed on to the bridge with an unsuspecting smile and shook hands warmly. Then he turned to introduce the two strangers who accompanied him. One was a tall, fair-haired man with a strong-jawed face that was handsome without being soft, while the other was shorter, fatter, and cheerfully ugly.

"Captain Armstrong," Van Eerden said politely. "I think that perhaps you know Mister Nicolson who is one of your company representatives from England. And this is a new colleague of mine, Mister Helders from the Dutch Port Control Authority."

Mark Nicolson and Dirk Helders advanced with equally disarming smiles and said hello.

# 16

AN hour before Detective Sergeant Harry Stone had radioed a report from a Dutch fishing boat that was drifting with nets cast in the North Sea. He had searched the decks and rails of the *Monolith* with powerful binoculars and found them unnaturally empty. It was a glorious morning and the supertanker had been six weeks at sea, and yet there were no cheerful faces awaiting their first glimpse of their home port. Even if every deckhand had a job below, the women and children should have been visible on deck.

Stone's report was enough to convince Nicolson and Helders, and so they and Van Eerden were not surprised when the pilot boat failed to receive its usual welcome. They pretended to notice nothing amiss as they ascended the silent ship to the bridge.

They found the Captain standing by the helmsman and Fraser standing forward where he could look down at the radar screens or watch ahead. The only other man present was Alan Spencer who stood just in front of the door to the radio room that was open by six inches.

Nicholson knew instinctively that the men who now controlled the ship would be hidden in the radio room. The door was partially open so that every word spoken on the bridge could be overheard. Probably there were hostages in there with guns at their heads, and almost certainly there would be a gun muzzle lined up through the crack in the door and centred on a point midway between the First Radio Officer's shoulder blades.

After Van Eerden had made the introductions Nicolson promptly took Armstrong by the hand, pumping it with easy familiarity.

"Hugh, it's good to see you again!

Apart from the hurricane and the vessel in distress, how was the trip?"

Armstrong was baffled by this total stranger who greeted him like an old friend, but he did not let it show. He cracked a worn smile and joked, "Apart from the points you mentioned, quite uneventful."

"Well, you've brought her home on schedule again, and considering the extra difficulties this time I think the company will be paying you a bonus." Nicolson was loud and jovial and he paused for a second before he added. "They sent me out to arrange the repatriation of these German sailors you picked up. If any of them need hospital treatment or medical facilities Mister Helders here can arrange it."

"They're all in good health," Armstrong said cautiously. "I don't think that will be necessary."

"Good," Nicolson laughed. "In that case we are only here to drink your gin."

"First we must dock the ship," the

pilot reminded them.

"You have command, Mister Van Eerden," Armstrong assured him formally.

While the Captain and the Dutch pilot discussed speed and course and all the complexities involved in bringing the *Monolith* to a safe berth, Mark Nicolson strolled over to Alan Spencer. He had studied the files on every man aboard and had recognized the First Radio Officer by the rank bars on his shoulders. Again he smiled and extended a hand with the relaxed air of an old friend.

"Hello, Alan, you're looking fit again. I can see you've acquired another Persian Gulf suntan."

Spencer was startled. It showed on his face but his back was to the radio room. Hesitantly he gripped the offered hand.

"You haven't met my friend, Dirk Helders," Nicolson continued affably. "Dirk was a superintendent on one of the northern dock basins but he's just

307

307

been transferred to the oil terminal. Dirk, this is Alan Spencer, he's an old friend of my wife and I."

"I am pleased to meet you." Dirk Helders spoke formally but a cheerful beam brightened his ugly face. They shook hands and then Helders turned casually to Nicolson.

"Mark, if Alan is an old friend why don't you invite him along tonight? Mark and his wife are joining my wife and I for dinner," he explained. "You would be most welcome."

"That's an idea," Nicolson was enthusiastic. "Bring Jackie along and give her a treat." He paused. "How are Jackie and the kids?"

Spencer was bewildered. He didn't know what was happening but he played the game.

"Jackie's fine," he said. "And the kids."

"They have three," Nicolson told Helders. "A boy and two little girls, How old are the twins now, Alan? They must be nearly four."

"We had a birthday party for them last week," Spencer said slowly.

"That must have been fun." Nicolson glanced at his wristwatch and then made a suggestion. "Look, it's going to be half an hour yet before the ship is berthed, and the Captain and the pilot are going to be busy till then. Why don't we go below and find Jackie. We can fix things up about dinner tonight, and perhaps persuade one of the other women to look after the kids for a few hours."

Spencer paled. He was sweating and he knew that the unseen man aiming a Schmeisser machine pistol at his back must be equally tense. He swallowed hard.

"I think we'd better wait. I — I might have to answer the radio."

"There'll be nothing now," Nicolson said confidently. He took the matter out of Spencer's hands by turning directly to the Captain.

"Hugh, can you spare Alan from the bridge?"

Armstrong wiped all trace of expression away from his face as he considered. All he knew was that this man who called himself Nicolson was not an official from the company, and that consequently the fat, ugly man who called himself Helders must also be an imposter. They were playing some gigantic game of bluff in which his ship and every life aboard was at stake. He could either assist them and throw the strain of the next decision on to the terrorists, or he could take the line of no resistance and refuse the request.

Fraser was watching intently. He was equally aware of what was happening, but there was nothing that he could say or do. The decision was for the Captain alone.

Armstrong was weary. Out of the past seventy two hours he had had less than twelve hours of sleep. The rest of the time he had stood on the bridge. His weariness was a vast dull weight spread over his body, and he knew that his Chief Officer had fared no better.

However, at the same time he knew that Bakarat and Takaaki were equally tired. They and their men had shared the same merciless hours of strain and tension. They were all nearing the limit of their endurance, and only these new arrivals were fresh and strong. Armstrong didn't know who these men might be, or what they intended, but they were a breath of hope aboard a doomed ship.

"I don't think you'll be needed, Mister Spencer," Armstrong said calmly. "If you wish you can take Mister Nicolson and Mister Helders below."

Spencer stood immobile, but Nicolson put a firm, comradely arm around his shoulders.

"That's settled then, Alan. Let's find Jackie."

Spencer moved reluctantly. Nicolson was pulling him forward and any determined resistance on Spencer's part would have been too obvious. Dirk Helders fell casually into step on Spencer's right and with Nicolson still gossiping merrily they began to leave the bridge. Now was the razor-edged moment when the terrorists had to chose. They could reveal themselves prematurely or they could allow the three men to depart. Neither Nicolson or Helders showed any sign that they were aware of the electrified air, while Armstrong and Fraser ignored the situation and gazed steadily ahead at the approaching Europort. A seagull screamed with a shattering cry as it passed the open door of the bridge, and the Sword of Damocles could have been suspended on a steel chain compared to the fragility of the thread on which hung the fate of the *Monolith*.

Hasan Bakarat stood just inside the door of the radio room with his shoulders pressed against the wall and his machine pistol in his hands. Through the narrow crack that he had left open he saw Spencer move away and he wanted to curse. There was sweat trickling down the side of his neck and his hands were slippery. He had to remember the tight time limit and the fact that the two unexpected visitors were of negligible importance. All that really mattered now was that the pilot be kept unsuspecting so that the ship docked on schedule.

Bakarat turned his head. He had Takaaki and Farraj behind him and at pistol point they were holding John Deverell and Anthony Gaye. He wished now that he had not split his men into three groups, for he had sent Shefik and the two remaining Japanese to patrol below and ensure that none of the crew showed any warning signals on deck. However, he decided that he and Takaaki could control the hostages and the bridge.

"Farraj," he whispered curtly. "Leave by the back way and follow them. When they are out of hearing you must catch them up. Take them to the saloon. Zakaria and his group must hold them and then you can return here."

Farraj nodded his understanding. He

took a firmer grip on his machine pistol and then backed out of the radio room and hurried below.

★ ★ ★

On the bridge Armstrong heard the muffled whisper and the faint movement. He was well aware that there were two exits from the radio room and he guessed what was happening. He felt helpless and prayed to God that Nicolson and Helders knew what they were doing.

Fraser also heard and guessed that the terrorist strength in the radio room had been reduced by one man. As yet he saw no room to hope but he carefully moved his position so that he and the Captain were on opposite sides of the radio room door.

The pilot was apparently deaf and blind to everything as he concentrated on his job, bringing the bows of the *Monolith* round in a great sweep that would bring her broadside on to the appointed jetty head.

Two powerful tug boats appeared, ready to make fast and help manoeuvre the ponderous supertanker over the last stage of the docking operation.

★ ★ ★

As Nicolson, Helders and Spencer descended the companionways from the bridge, Nicolson maintained his inconsequential one-sided conversation. They reached B deck and turned into the interior of the ship, guiding the faltering Spencer around the corner of an alleyway, and only then did Nicolson lower his voice to a soft murmur.

"We are police, Mister Spencer. We know you have a terrorist group aboard, but before we can act we must know where your women and children are being kept hostage."

"In the saloon," Spencer said quickly. It was suddenly a relief to know who these men were and his voice was quiet but steady. "But I think there's one behind us."

"I know," Nicolson had heard the quick patter of light footsteps coming down the second companionway behind them and so he did not look back. Instead he and Helders swiftly steered Spencer around the next corner.

Helders retained his grip on the Radio Officer's arm, pulling him along without pause, but Nicolson stopped and flattened himself silently against the bulkhead. His hand slipped inside his coat and he pulled out a Smith & Wesson automatic.

"I think you'll like my wife, Alan," Helders took up the conversation as they moved away down the corridor. "Gerda is much better looking than me, but of course that is not so difficult." He chuckled loudly. "Anyway, you will find that she is a good cook."

Farraj came round the corner fast. He was hurrying to catch up with the fading voices and he walked blindly into the waiting Nicolson. A hand snapped like a steel clamp on the muzzle of his machine pistol and twisted it violently out of his grasp. A shoulder crashed against his own and a knee smashed into his crotch with crippling force. All those things happened in the same split second and the black snout of an automatic was rammed into his throat.

"Be still, be quiet," Nicolson commanded, and the menace in his grey eyes completed the threat.

Dirk Helders came back at a run, his ungainly bulk moving with speed and precision. He scooped up the machine pistol before Farraj had drawn his first startled breath and the issue was no longer in doubt. With his free hand Helders pulled his own automatic.

"Can you use this?" he asked Spencer.

The Radio Officer nodded and took the gun. For the first time in three days Alan Spencer felt a glimmer of hope. He was still afraid for his wife and children, but if Bakarat was not stopped he felt sure that they would die anyway. The automatic gave him courage and he rapidly explained the situation on board the *Monolith*.

The women and children were the keys, Nicolson and Helders had guessed that long before. They listened with bleak faces as they inherited the terrible dilemma that had confronted the officers and crew.

"We have to attack the saloon," Nicolson said at last. "If it was just a matter of recapturing the ship and arresting the terrorists for past crimes, we couldn't take the risk. But it's got far beyond that now. If that warhead is primed and due to explode at one o'clock then hundreds of people are going to die, including the people on board this ship — and including the women and children. Whatever the cost, we have to stop it."

"I agree," Helders said heavily. "It is not possible to clear the area in the time available, and I do not think that this man Bakarat will allow the evacuation of the ship. He and his men must know that they are engaged on a suicide mission, and to ensure its success they will hold their hostages until the end!"

Spencer nodded slowly, accepting what he had feared. He was sick inside with worry for Jackie and the children, but it was no longer in their best interests to remain inactive.

"You're right," he admitted. "We must take a chance."

* * *

Elizabeth Fergusson had a practical and logical mind, and she had been thinking hard. She had recognized Sue Deverell's hesitant endeavour to tempt Zakaria for what it was and she had accurately analysed the reactions from Jackie and Jane. Afterwards she had reached the inevitable conclusion that there was no way in which the women could help themselves. Sex had proved useless as a weapon and in any case the mothers were too terrified for the safety of their children to endorse any move towards their own salvation.

They could not help themselves and so they could only pray for help from outside, but even so Elizabeth was not a woman to merely sit and pray. Her mind ranged over the possibilities of a rescue attempt, and the ways and means by which they could give some measure of aid to any would-be-rescuers.

The rescuers in her mind were her husband and the other engineers. She knew that Bakarat did not have enough men to keep a tight guard on the engine room and the lower regions of the ship, which meant that Arthur still had some measure of command down there and that he and his men had some freedom of movement. She knew that Don Campbell and George Darling would be frantic with worry for Jane and Mary and the children, but that Arthur would hold them in check until desperation was justified.

Everything was balanced on the scales of fear, but when the scales tilted and inaction was no longer a guarantee for their lives, then an effort would be made to free them.

Elizabeth was sure of this and she dreaded the moment, because men would die and perhaps in vain. She wondered how it would happen, glancing at the saloon doors and the door into the galley which were the only entrances. Then she realized that the women and children were scattered, blocking the lines of fire between the four Arabs and the two doors. She saw then the only way in which she could help.

Elizabeth stood up and went over to the window. The *Monolith* was still coming round in its great half circle and she could see the Europort ahead on the starboard bow.

"We're nearly there," she said, forcing an effort at cheerfulness into her tone. "I can see the oil tanks — and there's one of the tugs." She turned her head to offer a general invitation. "Come and see, the tugboat will soon be alongside!"

There was silence, but then Angus left his mother and went to the window.

"Where? Where's the tugboat?"

"Over there!" Elizabeth pointed and then lifted the boy up on to the chair beside her.

Angus saw it too. At the same time he saw another ship on the horizon which added to his interest. That was enough for three-year-old Ian who scrambled up to join his brother. Jane Campbell automatically followed her sons.

Elizabeth glanced back at the others. "It's something to look at." She pressed them as much as she dared.

Sue Deverell realized that the older woman was trying to tell them more. She stared into Elizabeth's eyes and began to understand. She stood up and lifted Stephen with one arm.

"Come on, you're always interested in other ships," she told him.

Jackie Spencer hesitated only a moment and then she brought the two little girls to join the group at the window.

They all stared at the tugboat and the ship on the horizon. Slowly interest waned and Elizabeth sensed that they were ready to disperse. "Let's all sit here," she said quickly.

She kept her tentative hold on Angus and Sue retained her hold on Stephen, effectively trapping the two mothers and the rest of the children. They all sat down at the table nearest the window and stared out.

Only Mary Darling remained in the centre of the room. She was silent and withdrawn. Her only thoughts were for the baby.

"Mary," Elizabeth called her after a few moments had passed. "Don't be unsociable, come and join us."

Mary looked up and realized that she was alone. She hesitated for a moment, half afraid to move under Zakaria's watchful eyes, then she went to the table by the window and sat with the others.

Elizabeth closed her eyes and prayed that Arthur and the others would not sacrifice their lives. At least she had manoeuvred the children out of the direct line of fire and she could do no more.

Five minutes passed. Zakaria leaned against the wall with his machine pistol in his hands and watched the double doors to the main corridor. Jabril struck an identical pose against the opposite wall and watched the door to the galley. The remaining two Arabs sat at a table with their weapons lying between them. One of the doors to the corridor suddenly opened.

Zakaria stiffened. Jabril's head turned sharply and the other two men looked up and reached for their guns.

Elizabeth Fergusson's heart raced with anticipated panic.

The Arabs recognized their friend Farraj and started to relax.

A blink of time elapsed, time for

Farraj to take half a step, and for Zakaria to realize that Farraj had fear on his face and that his hands were empty. Behind Farraj was a ship's officer.

Zakaria brought his machine pistol up again as the second half of the double doors was kicked open. Dirk Helders crashed through the opening with Farraj's machine pistol levelled in his big hands. The fat man was moving right and he had the advantage. Zakaria twisted to cover him and Helders saw the fanaticism in the Arab's eyes. With no further hesitation Helders squeezed off a short burst and cut Zakaria down before he had a chance to return the fire.

In the same blink of time Mark Nicolson had burst through the door from the galley. He saw Jabril swinging round to fire at Helders and the Smith & Wesson in his hand barked once. Jabril was slammed back against the wall with an accurate bullet lodged in his heart.

Helders bellowed a command and the remaining two Arabs froze and lived.

Spencer used the butt of his borrowed automatic to club Farraj viciously across the back of the head. Farraj fell sprawling and Spencer was free to run forward and comfort his wife.

Mary Darling had fainted but Elizabeth caught the baby before it fell from her arms.

With his left hand Nicolson had flipped out a hand radio from the top pocket of his jacket. He pressed the transmit button with his thumb and rapped curtly:

"Spearhead to Strike Force, attack now — *Spearhead to Strike Force — attack now!*"

# 17

ALEXANDER Gwynne-Vaughan received Nicolson's radio call as he stood upon the jetty head that was waiting to receive the *Monolith*. He spun on his heel, raised his right hand above his head and then flung it in a classic pointing gesture towards the supertanker looming large on the horizon. The signal was unmistakable and was acknowledged by the simultaneous roar of six powerful engines barking into life. Six sets of rotor blades whirled at speed and the combined wind pressure almost swept Gwynne-Vaughan into the sea. Then the six Scout helicopters rose from the jetty and howled like a cloud of avenging hornets towards the *Monolith*.

Each helicopter carried a pilot, four 0.50 inch machine guns, and five well-armed and grimly determined men of the *Marechaussee*, the Dutch military police.

★ ★ ★

On the bridge of the *Monolith* the short burst from the machine pistol, followed by the muffled bark of the Smith & Wesson, were both audible. Armstrong and Fraser exchanged glances, each recognizing in the other the same agony of apprehension. There was sweat in the creases of Armstrong's brow, and where his hands hung in low fists his knuckles gleamed white. Fraser could feel his heart pounding and his mouth was drier than the blistered sands that framed the Persian Gulf.

The helmsman turned his head slightly and bit his lip, and only the tubby little Dutch pilot seemed unconcerned and unaware. Van Eerden was still concentrating on docking the ship.

Fraser heard the door to the radio

room creak open and partially turned. He saw Bakarat standing in the open doorway with his machine pistol threateningly raised. There were patches of white on either side of the cruel hawk nose, and the first signs of fear and fury were radiating from his baffled eyes. Even before they heard the menacing buzz of metallic wings Bakarat knew that somehow he had been tricked.

"What is happening?" he demanded harshly.

Armstrong raised his binoculars from his chest and focussed them on the six black dots rapidly taking shape off the *Monolith*'s starboard bow. What he saw made him afraid and yet there was a grimly resigned satisfaction in his tone.

"They look like police helicopters," he said quietly.

★ ★ ★

Inside the radio room Takaaki turned his head to hear what was being said on the bridge. While his attention was distracted John Deverell and Anthony Gaye exchanged meaningful glances.

Each of the two junior officers felt some degree of responsibility for the events that had befallen the ship. Gaye was convinced that he shared the guilt of Philip Eldridge in bringing the terrorists to the *Monolith*. He had been in charge of the lifeboat's radio and had transmitted messages to Bakarat's orders, and after the event he could now think of a dozen ways in which he might have inserted a warning.

For his part Deverell could not forget that at one point he had held a rifle in his hands and had failed to use it. Perhaps he would have been killed if he had tried, but now he was sure that they were all going to die anyway and he did not want to die a coward.

Both men wanted a chance to atone, a chance to redeem themselves, if nothing else, a chance to die fighting.

★ ★ ★

Bakarat took two steps forward to get a better look at the descending helicopters and then he began to scream abuse. As if that were a signal there was a sudden, violent surge of movement within the radio room. A shrill Japanese cry of animal rage rang out above a shattering burst from a machine pistol as human bodies clashed in combat. Bakarat whirled towards the sound, took a fast step back towards the radio room and then realized his mistake.

For the past ten minutes Armstrong and Fraser had known that one of them must die. Their ship was nearly home and now that the pilot was on board to take command in the final minutes they were both expendable. Armstrong had noticed when Fraser had moved cautiously to the right and so he had stayed to the left. If there was a telepathic link between them it was in essence the need to save their ship from the ultimate horror, and so they were two men with one mind. When the first real opportunity came they were ready, each hoping that at least the other would survive.

"*Rush him, Mister Fraser!*"

Bakarat spun back to see the two men charging him from two opposing directions with a joint speed and fury that only death could stop. He had a split second in which to chose and the Captain's roar of command had tilted the balance, exactly as Armstrong had known that it would. Bakarat swung the muzzle of his machine pistol to the left and squeezed the trigger. The blaze of bullets hit Hugh Armstrong in the chest and halted him in mid stride. For a hairline of time he seemed to be suspended there and then his momentum was reversed and he was hurled back across the bridge.

Armstrong was dead but Fraser came on. Bakarat made a desperate effort to swing his machine pistol to the right, but then Fraser hit him with all the speed and force of an express train jumping its rails. Bakarat was carried back a good six feet and when he crashed over backwards to the deck Fraser's driving weight was still on top of him.

The machine pistol was torn from Bakarat's hands as he and Fraser rolled together. They hit the bulkhead and came apart, but sprang instantly to their feet. There was a demented madness in Bakarat's eyes that could only be matched by the vengeful fury in Fraser's heart. For a few moments they fought as only Hector and Achilles could have fought, attacking each other with fists instead of swords. Then Fraser launched his right fist in a savage upward swing that smashed at the underside of Bakarat's jaw and spun him in a full circle before he again toppled to the deck.

Bakarat had a broken jawbone but even in his agony he wad not defeated. His hand groped for the fallen machine pistol that lay on the deck beside him. Fraser dived forward as a single shot rang out and when he dropped on to the hawk-nosed Arab for the second time he found that he was attacking a dead man.

Van Eerden had turned from the helm, and in his right hand the Dutch pilot was holding an automatic. All his carefully controlled indifference had gone and now he was suddenly shaking like a man whose bones had melted.

Fraser pushed himself to his feet and then picked up the fallen machine pistol. Bakarat was dead and Armstrong was dead, but Fraser had no feeling for the Arab and no time to mourn for his friend. The Captain had not sacrificed his life so that his Chief Officer could stand idle in grief.

Fraser ran into the radio room with the machine pistol at the ready in his hands. He saw John Deverell sprawled unconscious on the floor. Anthony Gaye sat with his back against a bulkhead, his face white and his right hand gripping a shattered left shoulder that leaked blood in a steady stream.

Koiso Takaaki had vanished.

Fraser guessed that the Japanese

would be headed for the saloon. He too wanted to know what had happened there and he trusted to the pilot to assume command and hurried below.

He met Mark Nicolson and Dirk Helders ascending at a run.

"The women and children are safe." Nicolson stalled his questions. "And we've accounted for five Arabs. What's happened on the bridge?"

"Their leader is dead," Fraser said hoarsely. "But the Japanese group leader escaped. There are two more Japs and another Arab somewhere below — And there's a bloody great bomb in the central cargo tank!"

"We must attend to the bomb," Helders decided. "The terrorists we can round up later."

They turned on the companionway and hurried back down. In the same moment they heard the echoes of more gunfire.

"This way!"

Fraser forged past the two policemen and led them at a run along an alleyway. They came out on the open deck on the starboard side and were just in time to see the first helicopter wheeling away. The roar of sound and the wind pressure beat them back and the swinging tail of the helicopter almost touched the deck rails. When it was clear the three men pushed forward again to see what had driven it off.

Below them Shefik, Odusu and Yotaro had emerged on the main deck at the base of the superstructure and were blazing away at the descending helicopters with their machine pistols.

Helders leaned over the rail and fired down. Yotaro fell but Shefik and Odusu looked up and began to return the fire. Helders ducked back and the two terrorists took cover beneath the raised boatdeck.

Nicolson was looking forward. He saw a man racing up the length of the vast green deck, following the lines of black steel pipes.

"There!" he snapped.

Fraser looked and recognized the slim build and the glitter of spectacles. It was Takaaki.

Fraser lifted his machine pistol but hesitated. He knew what one spark could do down there where there were certain to be heavy explosive fumes leaking up from the oil tanks. The fury of bullets clanging and ricochetting off steel as they spurted from the muzzles of other weapons were an insane madness that he was powerless to stop — but he couldn't bring himself to add to it.

Takaaki was heading for the central cargo tank where the missile warhead hung suspended, but half way there he turned and blazed away with what was clearly his last clip of bullets. Afterwards he threw his machine pistol down and continued to run.

Another man ran out on to the deck in pursuit of the Japanese. From above Fraser saw that the man was a stranger with blonde hair and single gold bars on the shoulders of a creased white shirt. He realized that this must be the Third Officer from the *Rhineland*.

★ ★ ★

The sound of gunfire and the approach of the helicopters had brought Eric Weber rushing out on deck with Hayashi's machine pistol in his hands. He emerged on the port side of the island susperstructure only seconds after Takaaki had clattered down the port side companionways and started his frantic sprint forward along the main deck.

Weber paused for a second, staring up at the helicopters as they hovered just out of range. He realized that someone was shooting from the starboard side of the deck and started to circle the base of the superstructure. Then he saw the running man and recognized Takaaki.

Weber fired a warning burst that passed over Takaaki's head. The Japanese turned with bared teeth and answered with an erratic burst from his own weapon that hammered at the steel plates of the superstructure behind Weber's shoulder. Sparks, bullets and great chips of white paint flew in all directions, causing Weber to drop to his knees. Then the shooting stopped. Takaaki shook his empty machine pistol in a fury of rage and threw it away. He turned to run and Weber jumped up to follow him.

Weber might have shot Takaaki down as he fled, except that as he ran forward of the island he crossed the line of fire from Shefik and Odusu who were still crouching beneath the starboard boatdeck. Weber saved his own life by throwing himself flat on the deck behind the thick black pipelines running fore and aft. There he pulled himself to his knees again and shoved the muzzle of his machine pistol through a gap in the pipes. Takaaki was forgotten for a moment as he exchanged fire with the two remaining terrorists.

Weber had only one clip of ammunition

and it seemed that he had barely begun firing before it was empty. He huddled cursing behind the pipelines.

A helicopter swept low and close along the starboard side of the *Monolith*. As it drew level with the boatdeck one of the policemen on board fired an automatic rifle through the gap between the boatdeck and the main deck below. Shefik spun and died.

Odusu ran blindly, trying to find cover from the policeman in the helicopter. Weber had a clear aim but an empty gun. Then Dirk Helders again leaned out over the deck rail fifty feet above. The Dutchman fired and Odusu was smashed to the deck.

Weber sprang up, looking for Takaaki. The Japanese group leader had reached the access hatch to the central cargo tank. The hatch was closed but the clamps had been left unfastened. Takaaki grabbed the edges of the hatch with both hands and heaved it up. The weight of the suspended warhead made it heavier than before but by using all his strength he succeeded. The hatch crashed back and the heavy oil fumes swirled out on to the deck. The rope that held the bomb was exposed.

Takaaki looked round desperately. Two helicopters had already landed on the fore part of the long deck and armed men were jumping down. A third helicopter was landing just in front of the white island. Takaaki reached back with both hands over his left shoulder and grasped the hilt of his samurai sword.

Weber reached him with a flying tackle. The young German's shoulder crashed into Takaaki's hip and they went down together in a skidding heap. Takaaki lost his spectacles but he retained enough presence of mind to slam his elbow into Weber's face. Weber reached up both hands for Takaaki's throat and hung on, squeezing with all his strength. They rolled and cannoned heavily into a pipeline and it was there that Weber's luck ran out. He took the full weight of the impact on his injured left arm, splitting open the deep gash that had been caused earlier by Hayashi's sword. The sudden pain caused Weber to lose his grip. Takaaki drove a knee into his crotch and then broke free.

Again the Japanese reached for his sword. He pulled it clear from behind his back and looked dimly for the open hatch. Without his spectacles he was half blind but he couldn't mistake the raised black disc. The rope was a blurred line but he severed it with one deft swing of the sword. Then he turned and raised the samurai blade again to deal the death blow to Weber.

Mark Nicolson was running forward in the same moment. He dropped to one knee and aimed the Smith & Wesson with the barrel held steady against his left palm. Both hands were fully outstretched in front of him as he fired from a distance of forty feet.

The bullet struck Takaaki squarely between his tensed shoulder blades. The raised sword fell, but the hilt slid through his fingers and dropped behind him.

Takaaki collapsed into death.

★ ★ ★

In the vast, oil-filled cavern of the central cargo tank the released warhead was slowly sinking through its ninety-foot ink-black journey to the bottom.

# 18

FRASER and Helders joined Nicolson beside the open hatch and it was Helders who helped Eric Weber to his feet. Four of the helicopters had now landed amongst the pipelines on the green acres of the *Monolith*'s deck and the two remaining were hovering close on either side of the bows. The shooting had stopped and the armed Dutch policemen were swarming aboard the supertanker. A dozen of them rushed towards the four men grouped around the hatch, but then they faltered when they saw the frozen expressions of horrified anticipation on each of the four faces. Fear was real and monstrously alive in the very air and the police officers who came close sensed it and held back.

Nicolson stared at the cut rope that spelled the end. There was no action he could take and nowhere to run. The warhead was sinking beneath their feet and if it exploded on impact when it struck the bottom of the tank then the ship would erupt into one gigantic fireball.

Helders was uglier with dismay. His compensating cheerfulness had totally evaporated.

Weber dripped blood and felt faintly sick.

Two minutes passed and Frazer was the first to breathe.

"I think it must have hit bottom," Fraser said. "And thank God it hasn't exploded. The density of the oil gets thicker as it gets deeper and there's always a thick sludge on the bottom of the tank. The increased density must have slowed the rate of fall and the sludge must have cushioned the final impact."

Helders swallowed hard and then expanded his aching chest.

"Will there be time to dock the ship and empty this tank? We can perhaps pump the oil out to get at the bomb?"

Fraser glanced round and shook his head. The Europort which had once been on their starboard bow was now on their starboard beam, which meant that Van Eerden had turned the bows of the *Monolith* in a wide circle to head her out to sea again. The tanker needed almost unlimited time to make any manoeuvre at her present speed and there was no time left to make another change of course.

"If we can't get alongside the jetty then we must use the ship's pumps and pump the oil into the sea," Helders urged.

Fraser's mouth cracked into what was almost a smile. "There are laws against pollution," he said, "And there is another way."

John Deverell appeared with a message from the pilot on the bridge. He looked pale but unhurt except for a vivid bruise on his left temple. Fraser cut him short and said tersely,

"John, those aqualungs you and

Philip used to play around with in the Gulf — get them down here quickly. We've got a job to do!"

★ ★ ★

Within eight minutes they were ready to descend. Deverell had returned with the two aqualungs, wet suits, masks and flippers, and the Bo'sun had brought up a one hundred and fifty foot coil of rope. The two officers stripped and then dressed quickly in the hooded black rubber suits. They were helped into their harness and checked their pressure gauges to ensure that their air bottles were full.

"Are you sure you can dive safely in oil?" Nicolson asked doubtfully.

"It's been done before." Fraser was confident. "No one does it for pleasure but divers have gone down to release trapped valve wheels."

"All the way to the bottom?"

Fraser smiled wryly. "There has to be a first time for everything." He lifted

347

the double lines of corrugated air hose over his head and let them rest for a moment on his chest. He looked at Deverell. "Are you sure you're alright, John — after that crack on the head?"

"I'm fine," Deverell insisted.

Fraser tied one end of the rope around his waist while he gave his final instructions to the Bo'sun. He also attached a thin coil of forty foot line to his weight belt. Deverell carried a powerful rubber-cased torch although it was doubtful that it would be of much use. Both men fitted their face masks carefully, breathing through their nostrils to collapse the masks and thus check that they had a tight seal. Then they gripped the mouthpieces of the breathing tubes with their teeth and began to breathe from the air bottles.

Fraser led the way through the open hatch. His feet were clumsy in the swim fins but he found the rungs of the steel ladder bolted to the transverse bulkhead that led down into the oil. He descended into the black, viscous sea and when the crude oil closed over his head there was total darkness.

John Deverell followed him down.

They were blind in a lost world, two minute artificially-supported organisms in a flooded tomb where fish could not live and a cathedral could drown. The oil was blacker than the deepest bowels of any ocean, more silent, and clinging to them with a touch that was infinitely more slimy and evil. It seemed as though they were suspended in stillness and in time and yet they knew that time was running out. The grains of sand that were vital seconds were dwindling in number and there was no way to reverse time.

They descended as fast as they dared. Fraser found that once he had submerged it was easier to let his feet float clear of the ladder and pull himself down using his arms alone. He went down hand over hand, counting the invisible rungs and drawing comfort from the touch of each descending bar of steel. They were his lifeline back to the surface. Frequently he looked back and saw a dim suggestion of light above him. It was as though the light was shining round a corner up a distant tunnel, and yet he knew that the light was Deverell's torch and that the Second Officer was only a few feet above him.

The pressure increased with depth and Fraser had to blow through pinched nostrils to clear his ears. The viscosity of the oil became thicker and he felt like a fly clawing his sightless way down through treacle. He was breathing heavily and it seemed that his demand valve could not supply air quickly enough. He stopped to rest and Deverell bumped into him. They hung together for a few moments, unable to communicate, and then Fraser continued the descent. He realized that he had lost count of the ladder rungs.

After an eternity Fraser's groping hand pressed into a three inch layer of grease-like sludge that had the texture of vaseline. He had reached the bottom of the tank, ninety feet down. He twisted his body upright and waited for Deverell to join him.

Carefully Fraser tied one end of his forty foot line to the bottom of the ladder. The other end he passed through Deverell's belt so that it ran free and then he secured it to his own. Then they moved out together to search the bottom of the hold. The torch was useless for the beam failed to penetrate for more than a few inches. They could read a depth or pressure gauge by holding the torch to the glass but that was all. To find the warhead they had to grope across the sedimentary sludge with their hands.

They moved in blind half circles, radiating out from the foot of the ladder. Each time they touched the bulkhead they paid out a little more line before turning back to make a wider swing. It was a systematic method but it was slow and as they made their lengthening pendulum movements they swept the tank bottom with feet and hands in their efforts to make contact with the bomb. Fraser knew that they were immediately under the access hatch and he could only pray that the gentle roll of the ship had not deflected the free fall of the warhead too far from a vertical descent.

Five minutes passed, they had paid out twenty feet of line and then Deverell gave a jerk that brought Fraser back to his side. Fraser reached out his hands fearfully and felt the tarpaulin that protected the bomb. His heart beat fast as he untied the trailing rope from his waist and knotted it to the loose rope end that had been severed by Takaaki. He gave three sharp pulls to signal the Bo'sun on the deck above and then the slack was taken up and the warhead began its return journey.

Fraser and Deverell thankfully followed their lifeline back to the ladder and started their long climb.

★ ★ ★

Nicolson was waiting with a knife as the Bo'sun and his sailors lifted the dripping package out on to the tanker's deck. Deftly he slashed the ropes and peeled back the tarpaulin covering. Dirk Helders grabbed up the lethal suitcase like a relay racer taking a baton and sprinted to a waiting helicopter. The rotor blades roared and within seconds the helicopter was speeding out to sea.

The warhead was dumped fifteen miles out in the North Sea, five miles from the nearest ship, and with three minutes to spare.

★ ★ ★

The *Monolith* was safe and only then did Fraser remember that there was more.

"Bakarat said something about assassination teams hitting conference delegates," he told Nicolson hoarsely. "It was something to do with these talks between N.A.T.O. and the Warsaw Pact."

"We know," Nicolson said wearily. "We've stopped six teams along the Dutch frontiers over the past few days. We think we've got them all."

He could have said more. He could have told Fraser that they had only stopped one wave in an endless sea. Among the millions of hopeless refugees, the discarded nation of Palestine, there were thousands of Hasan Bakarats. They had different names, but there was no other way for them except to commit themselves to the same desperate road of hate and despair. While the camps remained men like Hasan Bakarat would flower amongst the filth and the terror war would continue.

Nicolson could have said these things but he said nothing. Only compassion and a new and humane breed of politicians could solve the problem of the camps, and he was just a policeman.

The *Monolith* was safe, and he was relieved to see the helicopter returning.

## A FOOT IN THE GRAVE
### Bruce Marshall

About to be imprisoned and tortured in Buenos Aires, John Smith escapes, only to become involved in an aeroplane hijacking.

## DEAD TROUBLE
### Martin Carroll

Trespassing brought Jennifer Denning more than she bargained for. She was totally unprepared for the violence which was to lie in her path.

## HOURS TO KILL
### Ursula Curtiss

Margaret went to New Mexico to look after her sick sister's rented house and felt a sharp edge of fear when the absent landlady arrived.

## THE DEATH OF ABBE DIDIER
### Richard Grayson

Inspector Gautier of the Sûreté investigates three crimes which are strangely connected.

## NIGHTMARE TIME
### Hugh Pentecost

Have the missing major and his wife met with foul play somewhere in the Beaumont Hotel, or is their disappearance a carefully planned step in an act of treason?

## BLOOD WILL OUT
### Margaret Carr

Why was the manor house so oddly familiar to Elinor Howard? Who would have guessed that a Sunday School outing could lead to murder?

## THE DRACULA MURDERS
### Philip Daniels

The Horror Ball was interrupted by a spectral figure who warned the merrymakers they were tampering with the unknown.

## THE LADIES
## OF LAMBTON GREEN
### Liza Shepherd

Why did murdered Robin Colquhoun's picture pose such a threat to the ladies of Lambton Green?

## CARNABY
## AND THE GAOLBREAKERS
### Peter N. Walker

Detective Sergeant James Aloysius Carnaby-King is sent to prison as bait. When he joins in an escape he is thrown headfirst into a vicious murder hunt.

## MUD IN HIS EYE
### Gerald Hammond

The harbourmaster's body is found mangled beneath Major Smyle's yacht. What is the sinister significance of the illicit oysters?

## THE SCAVENGERS
### Bill Knox

Among the masses of struggling fish in the *Tecta*'s nets was a larger, darker, ominously motionless form . . . the body of a skin diver.

## DEATH IN ARCADY
### Stella Phillips

Detective Inspector Matthew Furnival works unofficially with the local police when a brutal murder takes place in a caravan camp.

## STORM CENTRE
### Douglas Clark

Detective Chief Superintendent Masters, temporarily lecturing in a police staff college, finds there's more to the job than a few weeks relaxation in a rural setting.

## THE MANUSCRIPT MURDERS
### Roy Harley Lewis

Antiquarian bookseller Matthew Coll, acquires a rare 16th century manuscript. But when the Dutch professor who had discovered the journal is murdered, Coll begins to doubt its authenticity.

## SHARENDEL
### Margaret Carr

Ruth didn't want all that money. And she didn't want Aunt Cass to die. But at Sharendel things looked different. She began to wonder if she had a split personality.

## MURDER TO BURN
### Laurie Mantell

Sergeants Steven Arrow and Lance Brendon, of the New Zealand police force, come upon a woman's body in the water. When the dead woman is identified they begin to realise that they are investigating a complex fraud.

## YOU CAN HELP ME
### Maisie Birmingham

Whilst running the Citizens' Advice Bureau, Kate Weatherley is attacked with no apparent motive. Then the body of one of her clients is found in her room.

## DAGGERS DRAWN
### Margaret Carr

Stacey Manston was the kind of girl who could take most things in her stride, but three murders were something different . . .

# THE MONTMARTRE MURDERS
## Richard Grayson

Inspector Gautier of Sûreté investigates the disappearance of artist Théo, the heir to a fortune.

# GRIZZLY TRAIL
## Gwen Moffat

Miss Pink, alone in the Rockies, helps in a search for missing hikers, solves two cruel murders and has the most terrifying experience of her life when she meets a grizzly bear!

# BLINDMAN'S BLUFF
## Margaret Carr

Kate Deverill had considered suicide. It was one way out — and preferable to being murdered.